The COLOR
of
DESTINY

By
Julianne MacLean

Cover art design by Kim Killion

ISBN: 1491204052
ISBN 13: 9781491204054

Preface

⸱⸱⸱

Kate Worthington

According to *Webster's Dictionary*, destiny is defined as a predetermined course of events often held to be an irresistible power. I have often wondered if a person's life follows a path that is laid out long before he or she ever takes a first step. Or are we in control of what happens to us?

My name is Kate Worthington and I am a paramedic. I've seen some dramatic events in my life. I've watched people fight to survive, with impressive fortitude, and I've watched others surrender to death peacefully without fear of what lay beyond. Perhaps they could see what waited for them on the other side. Perhaps they knew it was beautiful.

Or perhaps they simply had no notion that they were in any danger to begin with, and simply allowed themselves to be carried along by fate.

I've also seen people come back from the dead, in more ways than one, and I wonder if they returned because there was some unfinished business to attend to. Maybe they still had lessons to learn.

I certainly have more than a few lessons to learn, but I do know one thing: Sometimes life is cruel, and at times it can seem rather pointless and tragic. But occasionally and surprisingly, certain hardships can lead us down a new path we never could have imagined.

And maybe that new path – that unexpected set of changed circumstances – was our destiny all along.

Saving Lives

One

I'm sure if you look back, you are able to pinpoint specific events in your life that changed you forever. For me, one of those events occurred on a country road in New Hampshire, in the frigid cold of a mid-February afternoon in 2007, when I watched a scuba diver pull a dead woman from the bottom of a frozen lake.

"What happened?" I asked the cop when I stepped out of the ambulance and felt the heel of my boot slip on a patch of black ice. *"Whoa."* I grabbed hold of the side mirror to steady myself.

"The driver swerved to avoid hitting a deer," he replied, blowing into his hands and rubbing them together to warm them. "Must have hit the brakes too hard. According to witnesses, the vehicle did a one-eighty, then rolled down the embankment. Landed upside down on the ice and stayed there for a minute or two before the ice broke. Then…down she went."

There were a few cars parked on the side of the road with their hazard lights blinking. It was the usual scene. Spectators stood around, watching the show. Cop cars were positioned with red and blue lights flashing, and other officers in neon yellow vests waved at oncoming cars, motioning for everyone to move along.

"How long has the vehicle been underwater?" I asked, not knowing if it was a single driver or an entire family with kids. Heaven forbid.

"About twenty minutes," the cop said. "Lucky thing there was a car following behind. Saw the whole thing and called it in."

"I don't know if I'd call any of this lucky," I said. "How did you get a diver down here so fast?"

"Another stroke of luck," the cop replied. "He's a volunteer with search and rescue, and conveniently, he lives right there." He pointed at a small lakeside bungalow.

"I suppose that *is* lucky."

"Yeah, though I'm not sure how much good it'll do. Twenty minutes under water. I'm not holding out much hope."

I strode closer to the edge of the road to get a better view just as the scuba diver re-surfaced. He bobbed like a cork out of a gaping black hole in the ice.

In his arms, he held the limp body of a woman.

CHAPTER

Two

I became a paramedic because I was fascinated by emergency medicine. This obsession began when I was sixteen. How exhilarating to imagine that I could actually save a life. I did briefly consider going to medical school, but didn't feel I had the grades.

Not that it doesn't take brains to be a paramedic. I studied hard to get through the program. On top of that, it takes a certain type of person to keep a cool head in out-of-control situations when people are covered in blood.

I'm proud of my skills. I'm also proud of the fact that I graduated from high school at all, when someone else in my situation might never have made it. I'll explain more about that later, but for now, let's focus on the dead woman.

As soon as the rescue team reached the snow-covered shoreline and set the body down, I checked for a pulse. There wasn't one.

"Hurry," I said. "We have to get her out of here."

I climbed up the embankment, reaching hand over hand, slipping on snow-covered rocks, while the rescue team followed behind me, awkwardly hoisting the gurney. They reached the road at last and extended the wheels. My partner, Bill, bagged and masked the woman while I began chest compressions, which I performed while walking alongside the rolling gurney as we wheeled her to the ambulance.

Bill always did the driving. He enjoyed blasting the horn, running traffic lights, and I'm pretty sure he entered this line of work because he loved the wail of the siren. Me…I always reminded him to slow down and drive with care. All I wanted was to keep my patients safe and tell them everything was going to be okay.

I knew this woman couldn't hear me, but when we slid her into the back of the ambulance and the doors slammed shut, I spoke the words to her regardless. "Everything's going to be okay," I said. Habit I guess.

"Buckled in?" Bill asked over his shoulder as he turned the key in the ignition. He was joking of course, because I had work to do in the back. I was busy putting the leads on and calling ahead to the hospital.

When I had the doctor on the line, I calmly and quickly explained the situation while looking down at the woman's face behind the oxygen mask. She was about my age, mid- to late-thirties, with dark auburn hair. Some of the ends were white with frost. She was a sickly blue-gray color, like a cadaver in a morgue, but also severely hypothermic. That observation gave me hope.

"What's her temperature?" the doc asked me.

I reached into my bag for the digital thermometer. "Eighty-one degrees. And she's soaking wet."

He paused, but only for a second, then began spouting off instructions. "Get her clothes off right away and cover her with a heating blanket. Tell your driver to crank up the heat in the ambulance as high as it will go. Start warm IV fluids. Stick the IV bags down your own shirt if you have to. The goal is to get her warm, even if you can only raise her temperature a few degrees. Don't defibrillate. Not yet. Focus on warming her up to at least eighty-six, then start CPR. We'll be waiting for you outside the ER doors."

I proceeded to remove the patient's wet clothes, then I wrapped her in an electric heating blanket and stuffed the IV bags down my shirt like the doctor suggested.

"Where's a microwave when you need one?" I said to Bill, shocked by the chilly bag against my skin. "Ooh, that's cold."

I couldn't imagine what it had been like for this poor woman, when gallons of ice water came pouring into her car.

I used my stethoscope to check for a heartbeat and looked at her face again. Would we be able to revive her? I wondered. And if we did, would she ever be the same?

"How you doing back there?" Bill asked as he took a hard right turn. I fell forward slightly, then tucked the blanket around the woman a little more tightly.

"We're okay. Do you have the heat up as high as it'll go?"

"Yeah, but do you really think there's any hope? She was down there a long time."

"She's not dead until she's warm and dead," I replied, taking her temperature again. Eighty-three degrees.

"Realistically, how often do they come back without any brain damage?" Bill asked.

"I don't know the stats, but I've seen it happen. When I was a kid, my dad took our dog hunting for rabbits one winter and accidentally shot her."

"Geez," Bill said.

"Dad didn't know that he shot her. He thought she ran off after something, then he found her in the snow after a couple of hours. I don't know how long she was dead, but we all got the shock of our lives when she woke up after my dad brought her home and laid her down by the woodstove."

"Are you sure she was really dead?"

"Yeah, a hundred percent sure. My head was resting on her chest. Maybe it was my body heat that brought her back."

"Sounds like a miracle to me."

I used my stethoscope to listen for a heartbeat again, but still, there was nothing.

"I don't believe in miracles," I said. "It's just science. No different from a frozen dinner that sits in the freezer for six months, then tastes great after five minutes in the microwave."

It was getting warm in the ambulance. I had to unbutton my jacket and shrug out of it. "How much further?" I asked Bill.

"We're five minutes away." He slammed on the brakes and laid on the horn. "Pull over you idiot!" Then he swerved and hit the gas.

I checked the woman's temperature again. It was eighty-six degrees, so I began CPR.

The ambulance doors flew open. I was dripping with sweat. Doctors and nurses surrounded us. Within moments, the woman was wheeled into the trauma room and the doctor yelled, "*Clear!*"

Bill and I backed out at that point, and I exhaled sharply, knowing it would take some time for my adrenaline to slow down. I was wired.

While I went to the tech room to type up my report, Bill offered to fetch me a cup of coffee, but I asked for a cold bottle of Gatorade instead because I felt like I'd just pumped iron in a sauna.

By the time I finished my report, our shift was at an end, but I made sure to check on the woman before I left. "Did they get her back?" I asked the clerk at the nurse's station.

"Yeah, they did. I was surprised because she was down for so long, but Dr. Newman just wouldn't give up. He kept checking her temperature and shocking her, then lo and behold, the heart monitor started beeping. You didn't hear everybody cheering?"

"No."

"Well, there were a few whoops and hollers. It really makes you think. Good job, by the way."

I moved behind the desk to toss my empty Gatorade bottle into the recycling bin, then went to the trauma room. It was empty. They must have taken the woman upstairs.

"Did she say anything when she came to?" I asked, because I couldn't seem to forget the blue pallor of her skin in my ambulance. It was like undressing a corpse. Which I suppose...she was at the time.

"No," the clerk replied, "'cause she didn't actually wake up. She's in a coma. They took her to ICU about ten minutes ago."

The hope and satisfaction I felt was immediately curtailed.

Maybe there was nothing to celebrate after all. Maybe it was just a matter of time before someone would have to pull a plug.

I wondered about her family. Did she have a husband? Children?

As I walked out of the hospital, a sudden wave of exhaustion washed over me. It's not easy to do chest compressions for extended periods of time, and I'd really wanted to bring this woman back. There were moments in the ambulance when I could almost hear her pleading with me to stay hopeful. *Don't...give...up.*

I unlocked my car and climbed into the driver's seat, then sat for a moment with my hands on the steering wheel. Staring straight ahead, I wondered if that voice in my head had less to do with saving that woman's life, and more to do with saving my own.

The house was dark when I walked through the front door, except for the eerie glow of the television in the family room off the kitchen. It flashed like a strobe light at a dance club.

With a heavy pang of dread, I set my purse and keys on the table in the foyer, shrugged out of my jacket, hung it on the newel post at the bottom of the stairs, and quietly made my way toward the kitchen.

I lived in an older home with a formal living room and dining room along the east side, but we had built an addition at the back, beyond the kitchen – a room for our flat screen TV and for more casual lounging about. I don't know why we thought we needed more space. It was just the two of us in the house. We had given up trying to have children a number of years ago.

I flicked on the light over the kitchen table, then stood in the doorway. My husband, Glenn, was asleep on the sofa. We had been together since ninth grade, and he was the great love of my life.

I still believed it to be so, even then, because we had been through some rough times in our relationship. Maybe that's why I was so tightly bonded to him.

My footfalls were silent across the wall-to-wall carpeting in the family room. I picked up the vodka bottle from the end table and checked to see if it was empty. Of course it was.

With a sigh of disappointment, I covered Glenn with the fleecy throw from the back of the sofa, though I knew I shouldn't be doing it.

I was a paramedic. I had seen this before. It was a mistake to cover an addict so that he wouldn't be cold, and it was a mistake to try and protect him from himself, even though all my instincts and the love I felt for him willed me to take care of him. Ours was a love not many of us are fortunate enough to experience, and before I tell you the rest of my story, I need you to understand that.

CHAPTER

Five

❧

1987

The first time I saw Glenn, my legs nearly gave way beneath me. It was as if I were being reunited with a lost loved one. I felt an inexplicable connection, though I couldn't fully comprehend it at the time. All I knew was that I was drawn to this person – both emotionally and sexually – and I wanted him in my life. How could I know, intellectually, that I was happy because I had just found my soul mate?

Yes, I now believe in soul mates. After everything I've seen and experienced, it's impossible not to believe it – but I am getting ahead of myself.

It was lunch hour during the month of October, and I was fifteen years old. My family had only recently moved from Canada, where I was born, to Bar Harbor, Maine, so my sister and I were the new girls in town. Mia was seventeen and a senior. She received most of the attention because she was tall, blond, and had perfect bone structure beneath a clear, dewy complexion. She was constantly told she should be a model, but laughed it off with a flip of her silky hair and an eye roll.

As for me, I wasn't unattractive. My hair was long, thick, wavy, and red, and there was nothing wrong with my bone structure and complexion – though I wore foundation to cover my freckles.

I wasn't as tall as Mia. She towered over me a good six inches, which usually made me feel invisible around her. Heads turned for Mia, while gazes whisked quickly over me. I wasn't jealous, mind you. I had my own friends and my own interests, and luckily Mom always made me feel beautiful. 'You are so pretty,' she would say to me when I arrived at the breakfast table dressed for school, or she might say, 'You are so creative,' when I painted a new landscape.

But let's get back to my story. The first time I saw Glenn…

I was sitting on the bleachers in the gymnasium with my new friends, watching pick-up basketball. We knew some of the boys who were playing, so we were there to ogle them, but as soon as my eyes settled on Glenn in his navy basketball shorts and baggy white T-shirt, I was captivated. There's no other word for it. Everyone else simply disappeared.

It wasn't because he was the most attractive boy, either. In fact, my friends didn't understand my obsession with him at all. Glenn was of medium height with a medium build. His hair and eyes were brown, and like me, he had freckles. His face wasn't exactly what one would call handsome. He had a rather large nose, but there was something manly and mature about him, and he walked with a swagger that made my stomach do flips and dives through flaming hoops.

I dragged my friends to the gym at lunch hour every day after that, and eventually Glenn began saying hi to us in the hallways. Even *that* was enough to send me into a swoon.

As luck would have it, we ran into him and a few of his friends at the mall one Saturday afternoon and hung out for a few hours.

Over the next few weeks my friends and I were blissfully absorbed into his older crowd, and were even invited to parties.

"So what's happening between you and Glenn Murphy?" Mia asked me one night while we were watching TV. "He's the one you like, right?"

"Yeah," I replied, "but we're just friends right now."

"Does he know you like him?"

"I think so. I mean, I haven't said anything, but sometimes he catches me staring at him."

"What does he do when he catches you?"

I shrugged. "He smiles at me. We talk about stuff."

I exhaled heavily. I won't call it a sigh because there was nothing dreamy about it. To the contrary, it was an expression of my frustration.

"I think you should tell him how you feel," Mia suggested.

She was a senior and had more experience with boys, but that didn't mean I had to take her advice.

"Umm. No," I scoffed. "That might work for you, but it won't work for me."

"Why? Are you afraid he doesn't feel the same way?"

"I don't know yet. We're all just friends right now."

She was quiet for a long time. "Maybe just turn the heat up a notch," she said. "There's a way to let a guy know you like him without actually saying it. You just have to look at him a certain way. Maybe lay your hand on his arm or his chest. Be flirty."

I chuckled, because I knew she was only trying to help. "There is no question that *you* have a special talent for flirting," I said, "but it's not my way. I don't want to wreck this."

"You won't. He likes you."

My gaze shot to hers. "Why do you say that? Did you hear something?"

She sipped her orange juice. "No, but you guys have been hanging out a lot lately. Obviously you all like each other."

Yes, but I wanted it to be more. My sister knew that, too, which is exactly what drove the wedge into our relationship three days later, when I saw something I didn't want to see.

The wedge came down at a party that got so out of hand, the neighbors called the cops to come and break it up.

It wasn't the sirens and flashing lights that started the tension between my sister and me, however. No, that particular incident occurred shortly beforehand, when everyone was still having a good time.

Naturally, the parents of the kid hosting the party weren't home. They had traveled to Jamaica for a week, trusting their seventeen-year-old son to take care of the house and water the plants. It became the running joke of the night. By the time two paddy wagons arrived on the scene, every plant-holder in the house was spilling over with beer. The floors were covered with potting soil from the runoff, and the dirt had been tracked up the carpeted stairs and into the bedrooms.

The music was blaring. I admit, I'd had a few drinks when my friend Janice took hold of my arm and said, "Come this way. There's something you need to see."

I followed her to the crowded kitchen. Janice pointed toward the sliding glass doors at the far end of the room.

There she was. My sister, Mia, throwing her head back and laughing. My stomach turned over with sickening horror when I saw that she was talking to Glenn.

They stood very close to each other in the corner. When she laughed again and laid her hand on his chest, my pulse began to race. I felt an intense hatred. I was filled incomprehensible rage.

Glenn was mine. She knew I liked him. Why was she flirting with him?

"I want to kill her right now," I said.

"Maybe she's talking to him about *you*," Janice replied. "Maybe she's trying to help get the two of you together."

At that moment, Mia grabbed hold of Glenn's shirt in her slender fist and pulled him closer.

They proceeded to French kiss for about six hours. Or at least that's how it seemed. I wanted to leave but I couldn't look away, though it disgusted me, because he was most definitely kissing her back.

"Let's go," I finally said, turning away and shouldering my way through the crowd. Janice hurried to grab our coats. She followed me onto the front lawn.

"I'm sorry," she said. "Maybe I shouldn't have told you."

"No, you did the right thing."

We started walking to her house, where – lucky for Mia – I was spending the night.

I apologize for telling you this story. It must seem trite and immature. That's how it sounds to me now as I recall it. *Boo hoo. My sister stole the boy I liked in high school. Woe is me.*

I realize that there are far worse things going on in the world. People are dying of terminal illnesses and starving in developing countries. But on that night, when I was only fifteen years old, the betrayal felt like a meat cleaver in my chest. I adored Glenn and I wanted desperately to be with him. It was a powerful desire, and nothing about it felt childish at the time.

To this day, I don't believe in that phrase: It's only puppy love. The feelings were real, and the agony was excruciating, because it had two prongs.

Glenn didn't want me. He wanted my older sister. And Mia was equally to blame. She had betrayed my trust and taken something – some*one* – she knew I wanted. I wasn't sure I could ever forgive her.

CHAPTER

Seven

"He's not right for you anyway," Mia argued the next day when I confronted her in the backyard. She was raking the leaves for Dad in exchange for ten dollars. She wanted to buy a purse she had seen at the mall the day before.

"How do *you* know?" I asked, folding my arms across my chest.

She wouldn't look at me. She kept her eyes focused on the pile of leaves she had raked into the center of the yard. "You're a junior, and he's a senior. He'll be gone after this year anyway."

"And so will *you*," I reminded her. "God willing."

I returned to the house and slammed the screen door behind me.

I will always regret saying that to her.

My friends and I didn't see much of Glenn's crowd over the next few weeks. The spontaneous invitations ceased completely. I suppose everyone knew it would be awkward between Glenn, Mia, and me, with all of us in the same room.

Glenn must have known I felt rejected, and I certainly couldn't stomach the idea of seeing them together. I hated to imagine that they were talking about me. Feeling sorry for me.

What exactly did they talk about on the phone every night? I couldn't fathom it. Glenn was into alternative music and books, while Mia was into the hit parade and shopping. It made no sense to me. I knew she was all wrong for him, and part of me couldn't wait for him to realize it.

My friends and I stopped going to the gymnasium at lunch hour to watch basketball. I often wondered if Mia was there in my place, sitting in the bleachers, cheering for Glenn. I didn't ask her about that. In fact, I didn't talk to her about anything. At dinner I stuck to small talk. Homework, chores, and whatever my parents wanted to talk about.

They recognized the tension between my sister and me, but thankfully they didn't force us to work it out at the table.

_____

"This will pass," my mother said to me one night while I sat at my desk doing homework.

I laid my pencil down on my math book and swiveled to face her. "No, it won't."

I hated the fact that I sounded like an emotional teenager, overdramatizing a situation that involved a boy.

But it was so much more than that. No one else realized it. At least not yet.

"You'll get over him," Mom said.

"No, I won't."

Her brow furrowed with concern. "You're only fifteen, Kate. There will be plenty of other boys."

"No, there *won't* be," I firmly argued.

Mom cleared her throat. I doubt she expected to encounter such strong opposition from me.

"And it's not just about that," I said, turning my back on her and picking up my pencil again. "It's about Mia. She knew I liked Glenn. Of all the guys in the school, I don't know why she had to go after *him*. She could've had anyone she wanted. Glenn was *mine*."

I stared down at the half-finished equation in my notebook, but all the numbers and letters appeared jumbled.

"Maybe there's a hint of jealousy, there," Mom gently said. "On her part, I mean. Maybe she needed to prove she was older and wiser, doing certain things first."

I swiveled again to face her. "Like what? Date a guy? She's dated hundreds of them. Okay, maybe not hundreds, but Glenn's certainly not her first."

Mom looked away and I regretted what I had said. I'm sure she suspected that Mia wasn't a virgin, but it didn't need to be announced at home with a megaphone.

For a long while we sat in silence. Mom had a habit of giving me time to ponder my words and reflect upon the hurt they caused. I did ponder them, and I was only sorry for how it hurt *her*. I didn't care how it reflected on Mia, because it was the truth.

"Someday," Mom said, "you are going to meet the most wonderful boy."

I held up a hand. "No. Please don't say that."

She stared at me, then nodded and stood up. "I'm here for you if you need me. If you ever want to talk about it."

Somehow I managed a melancholy smile, because she wasn't the one I was angry with. That honor belonged to Mia.

But not to Glenn. Looking back on it now, I wonder why I didn't blame him more for what happened. Why I made excuses for him.

Clearly, not much would change in the years to come, because once the drinking started, I continued to make excuses for him.

There are times when a feeling of hopelessness dominates our lives, but sometimes you just need to be patient. It's either not as bad as you think it is when anxiety is strangling you in its double-fisted grip – or perhaps it's about to do a one-eighty.

I remember the exact date of that sudden hairpin turn during ninth grade. On that night, the course of my life changed forever. Despite what you might think, I have no regrets.

How could I possibly want to change anything, because it resulted in a gift I cannot begin to comprehend all these years later, when I am no longer fifteen. I am now a grown woman, and I am grateful for what happened in my youth, no matter how difficult it was at the time.

But I am getting ahead of myself again…

His name was Jeremy. He was a friend of Glenn's, one of the guys who played basketball on the senior team. He had been at the mall that day when we all met, but I hadn't taken much notice of him, though he was better looking than Glenn. He was tall and golden haired with broad shoulders and a dreamy pair of blue eyes framed by long black lashes. Intellectually, I knew he was the best looking of the bunch, but for reasons I couldn't explain, I only had eyes for Glenn.

One night, the phone rang, and my dad called up the stairs. "Kate! It's for you!"

I had been lying on my bed listening to music, feeling sorry for myself. I remember the song. It was "The Killing Moon" by Echo and the Bunnymen – slightly alternative. Mia probably wouldn't know it.

"Hello?" I said.

"Hi, Kate, it's Jeremy. How are you doing?"

Immediately my heart began to pound, because Jeremy was a connection to those blissful few weeks with Glenn, when I had traveled in the same social circle. But why was Jeremy calling me? Did Glenn want to send a message? Had he realized Mia was not the right one for him?

"I'm good," I said with forced enthusiasm as I sat up on the edge of my bed. "How are you?"

"Great," he replied. "I hope I'm not calling at a bad time. You're not studying for a test or anything?"

"No, I'm just listening to music."

"Yeah? What are you listening to?"

I paused and shot a glance at my stereo. "Echo and the Bunnymen."

"Cool," he replied.

Another pause. My stomach started to turn somersaults.

"I haven't seen much of you these past few weeks," Jeremy said. "Where have you been?"

Maybe it wasn't as obvious to everyone else that I had a fanatical thing for Glenn, and that my sister had stabbed me between the shoulder blades. So I spoke casually. "I had a ton of projects due. Sometimes I wish the teachers would talk to each other instead of assigning all their stuff at the same time."

"I know what you mean. You have MacIntosh for English, don't you?"

"Yeah."

"Are you reading *To Kill a Mockingbird*?"

"I have an essay due on it next week."

"Are you finished the book yet?"

"I read it last summer, but I need to go over it again. MacIntosh wants us to pick a theme of our own to write about, but there are so many."

"It's a good book," he said. "Did you see the movie?"

"No."

"It's in black and white. It's good, but they leave a bunch of stuff out. It's probably best not to watch it until after you write your paper."

"I'll take that advice. Thanks."

I started to relax a bit. I inched back on the bed to lean against the pillows and headboard.

We talked about school and Jeremy's job at the grocery store, and what happened at the party a few weeks ago when the cops showed up. The guy who hosted the party was grounded for a month. I hadn't heard about that.

"So are you going to the dance next weekend?" Jeremy asked.

I felt my eyebrows pull together in astonishment. "I'm not sure."

Mia and Glenn were going. *Together.* She'd already bought a new pair of shoes. I wasn't keen on watching them hold hands all night and make out while they waltzed to some schmaltzy Air Supply song.

"Would you go if someone asked you?" Jeremy added.

I was completely bowled over. Did he have a thing for me all along? Had I been too blind to notice?

"It depends on who's asking," I replied, feeling very mellow and seductive.

"That would be me," he said with a chuckle. "It'll be a good time, I think. You want to go?"

After what happened between Glenn and Mia, I can't deny that at that moment my ego was a bouncing ball of satisfaction, especially because this invitation was coming from one of the best-looking guys in the school.

"I'd love to," I replied.

The whole world turned rosy red before my eyes.

He said he'd pick me up at seven.

The dance was still a week away, but Jeremy began an immediate courtship that impressed me greatly. He came to my classroom as soon as the bell rang for lunch each day and invited me to go for walks up and down the halls.

We would walk for a while, then linger in my classroom doorway, facing each other while leaning against the doorjambs. We chatted with other students who passed by.

My friends thought I was the luckiest girl in the world, but for me, the jury was still out on that point.

This may seem far-fetched. I still can't believe it really happened. It's almost comical when I think about it, but I assure you, this is how it went down.

I was in our garage the day before the dance, looking for a box that had gone missing when we moved to Bar Harbor. It contained some books from the old living room and a collection of 45s that belonged to me – yes, I am referring to the vinyl records. We still had a turntable with a needle, and I was very attached to my Springsteen *Hungry Hearts* single, and the *Eagle's Live* cassette, with the most perfect rendition of "I Can't Tell You Why" ever recorded.

The door that connected the garage to the kitchen opened on squeaky hinges, and Mia walked out to stand on the landing. She had just curled her hair. It was disturbingly bouncy.

"I need to talk to you," she said, resting her hand on the railing.

"It sounds urgent," I coolly replied while I continued to pull boxes from the shelving units.

"It is."

Honestly, I didn't want to hear whatever it was she had to say to me. An apology wouldn't make any difference. Even though I had a spectacular date to the dance, I wasn't ready to forgive her for coming on to Glenn at that party. It was an issue of trust. She was my sister. I had expected more.

"I don't know how you're going to take this," she said to me, "but I need to tell you how I feel."

I gave no reply, because I didn't really care. I was still so angry with her.

Then her selfish, earth-shattering pronouncement dropped like a bomb into the cluttered garage.

"I like Jeremy," she said.

Her voice echoed off the walls and bounced back and forth like a rubber ball.

Pardon the mixed metaphors, but I was in complete shock.

My hands froze over the cardboard box labeled 'more junk.' I turned to face her. "I beg your pardon?"

"I like Jeremy," she defiantly repeated, her gaze never veering from mine.

"You have *got* to be kidding me."

"No. I'm sorry, but it's how I feel. There's just something about him."

"Something about him?" I wanted to spit! "How about the fact that he's interested in *me*? Is that what makes him so attractive to you?"

When she didn't reply, I couldn't hold back the floodwaters of my wrath. "You have *Glenn*! Is he not enough for you?"

Mia shrugged her shoulders. Seriously. I wanted to strangle her until she turned blue.

Instead, before I committed a capital offense I would regret for the rest of my life, I swallowed hard, shut my eyes, and held up a hand. "Please don't say another word. I can't even talk to you right now."

Then I simply walked out and didn't look back.

⁓

Two days later, on the day of the dance, my sister acted exactly like the spoiled brat I had come to know. She called Glenn on the phone and told him she couldn't go with him to the dance because she wasn't feeling well.

As a result, I had two dates that night: Jeremy, who was doing the driving, and Glenn, who would ride in the back seat alone – because he had been stood up by my sister.

He was a good sport about it. Glenn, I mean. He didn't moan or complain about Mia's inconvenient illness. He was fun and easygoing, as always. He was the Glenn I had fallen in love with – the guy who always seemed calm and together, taking everything in stride.

When we arrived at the dance, we met up with the rest of his crowd and found a table near the stage with enough chairs for all of us. I was the youngest in the bunch, and it was only at that moment that it occurred to me that Mia might have resented the fact that I was infringing on her territory as a senior. Not that it mattered. I liked this group and they liked me. And really, what's two years as an age difference? It's nothing, once you finish high school.

Jeremy sat beside me and leaned close with his arm slung over the back of my chair. He asked me to dance every time a popular song came on.

Glenn didn't dance much. He stayed at the table, slouched low in his chair. I found myself talking to him a lot, however.

I liked Jeremy. He was a nice guy and incredibly good-looking, but I felt most comfortable around Glenn. I enjoyed our conversations. We seemed to share the same opinions about everything.

When a particular R.E.M. song came on, I saw Glenn sit up in his chair. I turned to Jeremy.

"Mind if I dance with him? Poor guy's depressed about my sister. He hasn't moved from his chair all night."

"Sure, go ahead," Jeremy replied. He seemed genuinely indifferent.

I tapped Glenn on the arm. "Want to dance?"

"Yeah," he replied, and we stood up.

The song was "Can't Get There From Here," and we danced with a circle of friends. As soon as it ended, a waltz started. It was "Wonderful Tonight" by Eric Clapton.

I was about to return to the table, but Glenn clasped my arm. "Dance with me," he said.

Butterflies swarmed thrillingly in my belly, but I fought to keep my emotions hidden as I moved toward him.

His hands slid around my waist and he pulled me close. My heart beat so fast I could barely breathe. All I wanted to do was hold onto him forever. I don't know why I was still so in love with him, considering the fact that he had been dating my sister for the past two weeks.

"How's it going with Jeremy?" he asked, leaning back slightly to look into my eyes.

"Okay, I guess."

Glenn glanced back at the table where Jeremy sat forward in his chair, elbows on knees. He was engaged in a conversation with one of his buddies and hadn't seemed to notice that Glenn and I were still dancing. Or if he had noticed, he chose not to acknowledge it.

"He's a good guy," Glenn said.

"Yeah," I agreed.

We said nothing more about Jeremy. We simply danced, but I was intensely aware of the feel of Glenn's shoulders beneath my fingertips. I slid one hand down, like a caress, to rest on his bicep.

His hand moved a little lower to the small of my back. He pulled me closer and I wrapped my arms around his neck.

Pulse racing, I daringly asked, "And how's it going with Mia?"

He didn't answer for a long time. When at last he spoke, his lips touched my ear and the sound of his voice sent a tidal wave of goose-flesh down the entire left side of my body. "I don't know, Kate," he said, "but I'm pretty sure I asked the wrong girl to the dance."

My heart turned over and my eyes fell closed, because he was telling me the one thing I had wanted to hear most – that he had feelings for me, and that he regretted ever becoming involved with Mia. In a way, I wasn't surprised. I had known she wasn't right for him. I just wasn't sure how long it would take for him to figure that out.

The song came to an end. Slowly, we backed away from each other, but he kept me there, locked in his gaze until the DJ played an upbeat song.

"We should go back to the table," I suggested, feeling shaken. He nodded.

We were both quiet for the rest of the night. Neither of us talked much to the others, but we made eye contact several times.

Jeremy hardly seemed to notice. He was a chatterbox, talking to the other guys, and when they played the last waltz he asked me to dance. Naturally. I said yes because I was his date. But each time I glanced back at the table, Glenn was slouched low in his chair, watching us with a furrowed brow.

CHAPTER

Twelve

I was confused that night as I lay in bed, staring at the ceiling. Mia didn't speak to me when I arrived home from the dance. She kept to her room, and I knew she was sulking over the fact that I had gone to the dance with Jeremy. I'm not sure what she expected. Did she want me to say, "No problem, I'll step aside?"

For all I knew, she had been flirting with Jeremy for days behind Glenn's back. Maybe Jeremy hadn't even wanted to take me to the dance. Maybe he was just fulfilling an obligation because he had already asked me, and it was too late to get out of it. Maybe that's why he hadn't seemed concerned when I danced with Glenn.

Mia could be talking to him on the phone at that very moment, I thought. Maybe they were plotting how he would let me down gently, so that he and Mia could be together.

Jeremy was a nice guy, but honestly, I didn't really care if he wanted to be with Mia. Not one small iota.

I was sound asleep the next morning when a knock sounded at my door.

"Kate, phone's for you!" Dad said from the hall.

THE COLOR OF DESTINY

"Got it." I sat up groggily and squinted through the beam of sunlight shining in through the white curtains. I rubbed my eyes and reached for the phone on my bedside table.

"Hello?"

"Hi Kate. It's Glenn."

The sound of his voice first thing in the morning was more potent than ten shots of espresso. I sat straight up.

"You're up early," I said.

He chuckled. "It's 11:00. Geez, did I wake you?"

"No, I was up, just lying here." I blinked a few times. "Actually, that's a lie. I was asleep, but I should be up now anyway. Thanks for waking me."

"You're welcome." I could hear a smile in his voice.

"Did you have a good time last night?"

"Yeah, how about you?" I adjusted the pillows behind me so I could sit up.

"It had its ups and downs," he replied.

I paused, wondering what he was referring to, exactly – the fact that he was dateless without Mia? Or the fact that I was with Jeremy?

"It was kind of that way for me, too," I replied, not giving away too much.

"Yeah?"

"Yeah," I said, thinking this was a very strange conversation. "So why are you calling me?" I boldly asked. "Shouldn't you be calling Mia on a Saturday morning?"

Obviously I was confident that something was happening between us, or I never would have asked such a question.

"I'm calling because..." He paused. "I was wondering if you wanted to go for a drive."

"I think my sister might have something to say about that."

There was another long pause. "We're not together anymore," he explained.

I threw off the covers and sat up on the edge of the bed. "Since when?"

"Last night. I called her when I got home, and I don't think she was sick. Do you?"

I shut my eyes and cupped my forehead in a hand, because I was filled with elation, yet I felt slightly guilty about that. I wanted to jump up and down and dance around my bedroom, but I had to keep it together and tread carefully. Respectfully. Even though Mia hadn't hesitated about stabbing me in the back, it just wasn't in me to be disloyal to her. Maybe that was naïve.

"I don't know," I said. "She looked kind of green at supper."

"Mm," he said. "Well, we both knew it wasn't going to work out. I'm sure she considers the past few weeks a big waste of time."

And do *you* consider it a waste of time? I wanted to ask, but I couldn't put him in that position. Not now. He was behaving like a gentleman, implying that it was Mia's wish to break up. Maybe it was. The fact that she went after Glenn at all still baffled me, because he was never her type and she told me point blank that she liked Jeremy.

It occurred to me in that moment that I hadn't given a single thought to how Jeremy might feel about this, but I wasn't even sure Jeremy and I were a couple. Sure, he asked me to the dance, but he hadn't even tried to kiss me. And *he* wasn't the one calling me this morning.

"Yeah," I said to Glenn. "Let's go for a drive."

CHAPTER

Thirteen

W hen Glenn picked me up at noon, I still hadn't set eyes on Mia. She never emerged from her room. I figured she was still sulking about the two guys who weren't coiled around her pretty little finger, though I wouldn't have been surprised if she dashed out the door and hopped into Jeremy's car at any given moment, without any thought to me.

Not that it mattered. All I cared about was spending the day with Glenn.

⎯⎯⎯

We drove to the beach and walked along the rocky shoreline. Though it was late October and the temperature was crisp, the sun was warm on our backs as we picked our way over the smooth round stones.

Later we sat on two giant boulders and watched the gulls float on the breeze, high above us against the clear blue sky. The tide was out and the water was calm. It was a perfect October day, one of the most memorable days of my life.

Glenn and I talked for seven hours straight. We talked about music, school, people, and life. He told me about his family – his older brother who was working as a clerk in the accounting department of a pulp and paper mill up north, and his older sister who had gotten married last year. Glenn was the youngest, like me, and he was close to his mother who was a nurse and a saint. His father, however, was an alcoholic and couldn't hold down a job.

We talked about our futures and what we wanted to do after high school. Glenn was interested in teaching because he liked the idea of lengthy summer vacations for the rest of his life.

I told him I didn't know what I wanted to do, and he said I'd figure it out eventually. Something would happen to me, and a light bulb would go off. I just hadn't found my calling yet. That was all.

He was so right about that because something *did* happen. It's why I became a paramedic.

After that first day together, Glenn and I were inseparable. I never imagined I could feel so close to another human being. I wanted to be with him every minute of the day. When I was with Glenn, I felt like I was my true self. No one understood me like he did.

We knew each other's schedules at school and walked together between classes, and sometimes wrote long letters to each other when we were bored during lectures and the teacher's back was turned. We held hands after school until the very last minute when it was time to part ways and board different buses. Then we would talk on the phone each night for at least an hour.

He was my best friend and I trusted him completely. He loved me with his whole heart and I loved him in return with equal measure. Though we were only fifteen and seventeen, ours was a passionate and mature love. I had never experienced such happiness and intimacy with anyone.

But you're probably wondering about Mia, and how we continued as sisters. Frankly, after everything that happened, I'm surprised we didn't scratch each other's eyes out, but our quarrel remained low-key. First, there was a mutual silent treatment for about three weeks, until Mia, true to form, took an interest in a waiter who worked at a local restaurant. He was impossibly gorgeous with wavy, jet-black hair and blue eyes. His name was Mark, and he was in an engineering program in university. As soon as she fell for him, all was forgotten, and our relationship returned to normal.

I never knew what happened between Mia and Jeremy. She never mentioned him again. He simply faded out of my life. He and Glenn remained civil, but Glenn spent most of his time with me anyway, and we preferred to be alone, just the two of us, at my place or his, so the popular crowd simply went on without us.

Mia dated Mark for six months, then they broke up and she made plans to move to New York and pursue a career in fashion. Sadly, that didn't work out for her, but I'll explain why later. All you need to know for now is that she played an important role in my life when I desperately needed my big sister.

Let me tell you about that.

CHAPTER

Fourteen

⸎

Glenn and I had been together for just over a year when everything spun out of control.

I should begin by confessing that I was no longer a virgin at that point, though we certainly didn't rush into anything. For five long months we did what all teenagers do. We fooled around in the backseat of Glenn's car or in my basement when no one was home. But I wanted it to be special, and though it might seem strange to younger readers in this day and age, I wanted to wait until we were married. That's how things were back then.

It's not as if Glenn and I didn't talk about it. The first time it came up, I was only sixteen.

"I love you," he whispered in my ear one night as we lay on a blanket in the field behind his house, gazing up at the stars.

I wrapped my legs around his until I was entwined with him like ivy on a trellis. I kissed his cheek.

"I love you, too. More than anything. I don't want this to ever end."

"It won't," he said, "because I'm going to marry you."

I drew back slightly. "What did you say?"

There was no laughter in his eyes, only love and desire. I was overcome by a rush of joy.

"You heard me."

"I want to marry you, too," I replied, because I couldn't imagine my life without him. To exist without Glenn would be to exist without the sunrise each day. Without oxygen in the air.

It sounds corny, I know, but they were the romantic beliefs of a young girl swept away by the passion of first love. It was shimmering and wonderful, yet agonizingly painful at the same time because we had to wait so long to truly be together. An eternity, it seemed. Why couldn't we just be free to lie together, to share a bed, and wake up in each other's arms?

The idea of such a thing stirred my teenage heart's desires and frustrated me immensely, for I was sixteen and living under my father's roof. He had strict rules. Glenn wasn't even permitted to enter my bedroom.

The first time my parents came home and found us alone together in the house we were sitting on the living room sofa listening to records. Dad went ballistic. He sent Glenn home and grounded me for a week.

"Teenage boys only want one thing," he told me. "You can't invite that boy – or *any* boy – over unless someone is home."

"There won't be any other boys," I argued in my defense, but my father looked at me as if I were a fool.

Two months later, Mom and Dad surprised Glenn and me by going out one afternoon and leaving us completely alone. They even asked us to lock the door behind them.

I suppose, by then, they had grown to trust Glenn. I could see it in their eyes when they talked to him, and in the way my mother smiled at me at the dinner table whenever his name came up.

"That Glenn is a very good catch," she said to me, leaning close to speak privately.

"I know, Mom," I replied with a sense of pride and relief. I was pleased they finally saw what I saw.

The next day, my mother nudged me in the ribs at the front picture window and said, "Didn't I say he was a good catch?"

My dreamy boyfriend had offered to mow the lawn one weekend when Dad was away at a professional conference.

"You don't need to convince me," I replied with a laugh, "but I'm glad you think so."

We watched him for a few minutes, then I laid my head on my mom's shoulder. She raised my hand to her lips and kissed the back of it.

It was one of those special moments I will never forget. I loved my mother with every piece of my soul.

Now, I only wish that perfect feeling of bliss had lasted a little longer.

A s I mentioned before, Glenn and I were together for five months before I gave him my virginity. I say 'gave' because I can't bring myself to use the word 'lost.' It's simply not accurate. There was no feeling of loss on my part, only a deep and meaningful satisfaction, without regret.

Glenn waited a long time for me to be ready, and he would have waited forever if I'd asked him to. I knew how much he loved me.

As it turned out, we didn't actually plan for my deflowering. There were no candles, or rose petals placed between the sheets in anticipation of such a momentous event. It was just like every other time we fooled around in his bed when his parents weren't home. The only difference was that I didn't tell him to stop when our clothes came off.

It all happened very naturally.

I won't try to paint it with a soft brush, however. It was excruciatingly painful, but I didn't mind because I loved him.

We were lucky that day. We were lucky for most of that year, in fact, because we took a few chances, and I wasn't on the pill.

I know now that I should have gone to the doctor and gotten a prescription for birth control, but the world was different back then. If you were a sixteen-year-old girl, you made sure no one knew you were having sex.

It wasn't unusual for my periods to be late, even as much as two weeks. My monthly cycle had always been unpredictable, so I barely noticed the following spring when I skipped a period – until I woke one morning, sat straight up in bed and struggled to remember when I'd last menstruated.

I should have been keeping better track of those things under the circumstances, but what can I say? I didn't think anything like that would ever happen to *me*.

When I arrived at school and stepped off the bus, Glenn was waiting for me at the curb. "You're late," he said with a smile.

My stomach turned over. "What did you say?"

"I've been waiting here for ten minutes," he explained. "What happened? Did your driver fall asleep at the wheel?"

I numbly placed my hand in his and allowed him to lead me along the paved sidewalk. "No, but I need to talk to you."

We had at least fifteen minutes before the first bell, and I had to get this off my chest. The stress was killing me and Glenn was the only person I trusted with this secret.

We headed toward a picnic table around the back of the school. We dropped our book bags and sat down. There was a chill in the air; I could see my breath, but the early morning sun was blinding. I had to squint. Glenn frowned at me.

"What's the matter?"

Of course he would know something was wrong. He could read my moods like no one else.

"My period's late," I bluntly said.

Glenn's eyebrows pulled together. "How late? A few days?"

I swallowed uneasily. "I'm not sure. I haven't been keeping track, but I think it's been at least seven weeks since the last one."

Glenn squeezed both my hands in his. "I thought we were being careful."

"We were," I replied. "We didn't take any chances last month. I don't know how it could have happened."

His eyes lifted. "Maybe it didn't. You said you weren't keeping track, and you're always late. Aren't you?"

I took a deep breath and let it out. "It's been a long time. Unusually long."

"Can we find out for sure?" he asked. "Can we get a test from the pharmacy? Or is it too early to tell?"

There was no Internet back then, no way to Google the answer to a question like that.

"I'm not sure. We should go at lunchtime and see what it says on the box. Do you have any money? I brought what I could. I have ten dollars."

"I have twenty. Will that cover it?"

"I don't know." My heart was racing and I felt sick to my stomach.

The bell rang. It was an abysmal sound because it meant we had to go to class and be apart until noon. How was I going to get through the morning?

W e bought the pregnancy test during our lunch hour, and let me tell you, it was the most stressful thing I'd ever done. First we had to linger in the feminine products aisle, searching for the right box while keeping an eye out, hoping no one from school would come along and discover what we were looking for. It was a small town and there was no way to remain anonymous.

When we found what we were looking for, Glenn agreed to take the box to the cashier while I discreetly slipped out to wait for him on the street corner.

He handed me the plastic bag and I shoved it deep into my purse.

"I'll do it right after school," I said.

We were so shaken by the experience that we spoke not a single word on the way back to school.

The bus ride home seemed to last forever. Thankfully, no one sat beside me, which was exactly how I wanted it, but it left me no choice but to stare out the window and imagine the worst-case scenario.

If the test was positive, how would I ever find the courage to tell my parents? My father especially. What would they say? And what would they think of Glenn? No doubt, Dad would place all the blame on him. He had certainly warned me enough. 'Boys that age are only after one thing...'

I felt sick and nauseous at the mere thought of it. God, it was going to be rough. But that wasn't the worst of it. What about the next nine months? I was in the tenth grade. What would my teachers think if I came to school with a belly the size of a basketball? I was a good student. A good girl. I couldn't bear to imagine it.

Two hours later, I stood in front of the mirrored medicine cabinet in the upstairs bathroom and read the test results.

God help me.

My knees buckled. The next thing I knew I was sitting on the fuzzy blue bathmat, staring dazed and wide eyed at that plastic white stick.

No. It couldn't be true. There had to be some mistake. I couldn't possibly be pregnant. Not me.

I dropped the stick on the floor, covered my face with both hands, and took a deep breath. I needed to think this through.

Though I was in a state of shock and panic, I did not cry or fall to pieces. I remained outwardly calm and picked up the stick and the rest of the packaging – heaven forbid if my father should come in later and find it on the floor.

Then I went quickly to my room to call Glenn.

Glenn met me an hour later at the public park in town. He had biked all the way there and was out of breath and perspiring when he leaped off his bicycle. Pulling me into his arms, he said, "I love you, and no matter what happens, I'll be right here beside you, and in front of you with a big stick if I have to be. Everything's going to be okay. I promise. As long as we're together, that's all that matters."

In that moment I realized there was no ceiling on what existed between us. He was my partner, my dearest, most trusted friend, and we were in this together, come hell or high water. I believed him when he said he would be at my side, and that gave me the strength I needed to survive anything...*everything* that was about to come our way.

❧

The first matter of business was to break the news to my parents. Maybe I should have told Mia first and asked for her advice, gained her support, but we had grown apart since Glenn and I started seeing each other. So, when it came time to sit down with Mom and Dad and spill the news onto the table like a heavy can of nails, I was on my own, with only Glenn at my side.

"Mom. Dad. We have something to tell you." My heart nearly burst out of my chest. After a brief pause, I said, "I'm pregnant."

Glenn squeezed my hand under the table.

Mom and Dad stared at me in disbelief for a full ten seconds. They did not look at Glenn.

"Are you sure?" Mom asked.

"Yes," I replied. "I took a test from the pharmacy."

"Have you been to see a doctor?" she asked.

"No, not yet, but I don't need to see anyone to know it's true."

My father sat forward in his chair. "You can't trust those over-the-counter tests," he said. "You need to see a doctor."

"I'll see one as soon as you want," I replied, "but it won't make any difference. I'll still be pregnant."

No one said anything, and the silence had weight, like a giant sack of wet sand on my shoulders.

Though my father was strict, I had never feared him before. Not until that moment when his eyes darkened with rage and his fists clenched and unclenched on top of the table.

"What do you have to say for yourself?" he said to Glenn. "Are you proud of this? Do you have any idea what you've done?"

"I love your daughter," Glenn replied, "and I'm sorry for this. We didn't plan for it to happen."

"Well, that's obvious!" Dad shouted. "You didn't plan for anything! You were reckless, selfish, and irresponsible! Just like your father."

Dad stood up and knocked his chair over onto the floor.

Mom clasped his hand. "Please, Lester, sit down. Let's hear them out. We need to decide what we're going to do."

My blood grew hot and sped out of control through my veins. I was terrified Dad was going to leap across the table and beat Glenn to a pulp.

At the same time, I was infuriated. Glenn and I were in love. He was nothing like his alcoholic father. It was *my* life, and I would run away and marry him before I would let my father separate us.

To my immense relief, he sat back down and worked hard to calm himself. His chest heaved and a muscle twitched at his jaw, but he didn't throw any punches.

"How could this happen?" he asked.

My mother covered his hand in hers. "I don't think there's any point in discussing that. We all know how it happened."

Her eyes bored into mine. I felt ashamed.

"Why didn't you come to me sooner?" Mom asked. "I would have taken you to the doctor, Kate. We could have prevented this."

I lowered my gaze. "I didn't want you to know."

"Well," Dad said, "the whole town is going to know soon enough – when you're walking around with a..." He stopped himself.

The neighbor's dog barked savagely outside at something. I wanted to run out the door and escape all of this.

Glenn sat forward. "I want you to know that I love your daughter, and I'll marry her tomorrow if it will make things right. I can increase my hours at the grocery store and support us."

A wave of love moved through me, and I squeezed his hand.

My father scoffed with derision. "If you think I'm going to let my daughter marry *you*, you have another think coming. And do you really believe you could support a family by packing groceries? Honest to God. You'll ruin everyone's lives, if you haven't already."

"Dad!" I couldn't let him talk to Glenn that way. "This is just as much my fault as it is his. You can't blame *him*."

"I blame both of you," Dad coldly spat.

My heart broke at the sight of his disgust. I was no longer his smart, clever daughter. I was ruined. Dirty. Soiled by teenage sex. That's what he thought. I could see it in his eyes.

I had no idea what the law said about teenage marriage. I was only sixteen. Could we get a license without my father's consent? I certainly hoped so, because that was all I wanted – to walk out of there with Glenn at my side and make our own way in the world. We could get an apartment and be together forever. We would be happy, loving parents. That's what my heart wanted.

Yet the sensible, more prudent side of my brain knew it could not be that easy. Glenn would have to quit school and so would I. He would never become a teacher. I wouldn't go to college and enrol in a program I had yet to decide upon. I wasn't stupid. I knew we would struggle financially, and those struggles would eventually bring stress down upon us. What if, down the road, Glenn grew to resent me for taking away all his choices?

He had so much potential. We both did. I wanted us to be happy and fulfilled. Was any of that even possible if a teenage pregnancy shifted everything out of order, created chaos, and crushed all our dreams?

I tried hard to think rationally, but in the end, all that mattered was my wild, mad love for Glenn. I wanted to spend the rest of my life with him, yet I had no real knowledge of the world outside my little bubble of romance. I didn't know that disappointment and grief could become all consuming. I couldn't comprehend how those feelings could cripple a person permanently and cast a shadow over an entire future.

Unfortunately, in time, I would learn more than I ever wanted to know about that.

Eighteen

I n the days following that dreadful conversation under the bright light at our kitchen table, my parents decided that my best option was to have an abortion. It was the *only* option, they said. Glenn and I weren't capable of supporting a child. Clearly trying to do so would ruin our lives. They argued that with a baby, I wouldn't be able to finish high school. Neither of us would go to college. My reputation would be ruined. The shame would be momentous, and that was a major factor in the decision. My father was an elementary school principal, and he dreamed of being superintendent of all schools eventually. He was ambitious. In those days, my scandalous pregnancy would ruin everything. We would be forced to move to another town and start over.

Move? No, no, absolutely not. That was out of the question. Leave Glenn? I couldn't imagine it. He was every breath in my body, the very life in my veins. Anything but that.

So we would stay, my father said, as long as I agreed to the abortion, which would solve this problem. Rub it out as if it had never existed. 'None of us would ever so much as *mention* it again,' Dad said. We would put it behind us and move forward. Everything would return to normal.

But was any of this normal? I asked myself as I got into the car to drive to the hospital on the day of the procedure. Would it be normal to pretend that something never happened when it did? Would it be normal to spend the rest of my life wondering what my child might have looked like? What he or she might have accomplished?

What if I was purging a genius from my womb? What if this tiny embryo might grow up to discover a cure for cancer?

All these questions spun around in my brain like a tornado, and I could barely think straight. What I needed was time. Time to make a decision, to explore what was important to me, but my parents had convinced me there was no time to think. If I was going to have the abortion, I needed to have it right away, or it would be too late. I was pushed and shoved and pressured into believing that it was the right decision. I was not given the chance to listen to my own heart.

Then, just as we were backing out of the driveway, Mia hopped into the back seat of the car beside me. "I'm coming with you," she said. She sat next to me in silence, then took my hand and looked me straight in the eye with an intensity I had not seen before.

Nineteen

Looking back on that day, I will always wish I had been stronger, more decisive, and not so easily influenced by what my parents wanted, for I had allowed them to talk me into something I was not comfortable with. The only reason I have forgiven myself is because I was so young, and I had been brought up in a home where my father set the rules, and we were expected to obey them.

He did not come with us to the clinic that day. I believe as soon as we pulled out of the driveway, he considered the problem dealt with. But he was unaware of the turmoil in my heart, which could not be dealt with so easily.

I sat in the waiting room staring at the posters on the walls. One explained the importance of prenatal vitamins. Another showed a mother in a rocking chair, bottle-feeding her baby and looking wonderfully fulfilled.

Magazines were stacked tidily on the tables, but I couldn't read because I felt nauseous – especially when my gaze fell upon the pregnant woman sitting across from us. She must have been in her last trimester because she was as big as a barn. I watched her rub her hand in graceful, soothing circles over her belly.

My nausea was mostly a result of morning sickness, but it was intensified by stress and the unthinkable fact that I was about to have my womb scraped clean.

I couldn't figure out how my mother could sit calmly in the chair next to me, reading a mystery novel, as if we were there for a routine flu shot.

Mia sat on the other side of me, chewing gum. "Are you okay?" she quietly asked.

I swallowed hard, to keep my breakfast down. "Not really."

"You don't look so good. Are you going to be sick?"

I didn't want to open my mouth to speak, so I simply nodded.

With impressive authority, Mia stood. "Come with me. The washroom is this way."

My mother looked up from her novel.

"She's not feeling well," Mia explained. "I'm taking her to the bathroom."

I felt everyone's eyes follow me – and judge me – as we hurried down the hall. By now the situation was urgent and I pushed through the door, not even bothering to turn on the lights before I bent over the toilet and retched up the contents of my stomach. Only vaguely was I aware of Mia flicking on the fluorescent lights, closing and locking the door behind us, and holding back my hair.

I hadn't eaten much for breakfast, so I was cursed with a violent spell of dry heaves. When I finished, Mia pulled a tissue from the box on the back of the toilet and handed it to me. I used it to wipe the tears from my eyes and blow my nose.

"Feel any better?" she asked.

I nodded, then closed the lid on the toilet and sat down. I rested my elbows on my knees, my forehead on the heels of my hands.

"Are you sure this is what you want?" Mia asked.

I looked up at her. "Do I have a choice? I'm sixteen and pregnant."

"You *do* have a choice," she said. "It's your body."

"But I already agreed to this. I told Dad —"

"It doesn't matter what you told Dad," she firmly said. "You can change your mind if you want to. I just don't want you to have any regrets."

She backed up against the door while I stood to splash water on my face. I pulled a square of paper towel from the dispenser, and patted my mouth dry.

"What does Glenn think?" she asked.

"He feels the same way I do."

"And how is that?"

"Lost. Uncertain." I dried my hands, crumpled up the paper towel, and threw it into the trashcan. "But he said he'd support me, no matter what I decided."

"Even if you decided to keep the baby?" she asked.

I looked at her directly. "Yes. He said he'd marry me tomorrow if that's what I wanted."

"Is it?"

I took a deep breath and let it out. "Part of me does. My heart wants it, but my head tells me it would be a mistake to rush into something like that. I do want to marry him, but we're too young. I'm afraid of how it could turn out. And Dad is right about one thing. We couldn't support ourselves, and I don't want to hold Glenn back. He wants to go to college, and so do I. I don't want him to be a grocery store clerk for the rest of his life. And when we have a child, I want to bring that child up right." I laid a hand on my belly. "Maybe I'm too practical, but I don't believe that love is enough. It might be at first, but I'm afraid all the hardships and money problems will eventually chip away at our love, and we'll grow to hate each other. Then we'll get a messy divorce and our kid will be totally screwed up."

I turned to look at myself in the mirror. "God, I'm a mess." I was the color of wet cement in a bucket.

"It's stress," Mia said. She unzipped her purse. "Here, put on some lip gloss. It'll make you feel better."

"Really?" I replied skeptically. Only Mia could suggest that lip gloss could cure the woes of a pregnant teenager.

When we returned to the waiting room, Mom looked up from her book. "What took you so long?"

"What's the matter?" Mia asked. "Were you afraid she changed her mind and tried to climb out the bathroom window?"

"That's not funny, Mia."

Just then, a nurse with a clipboard entered the waiting area. "Kate Worthington?"

"She's right here," Mom said, stuffing her book into her purse and rising to her feet.

She followed me toward the door that led to the examination rooms, but I stopped and turned to face her. "I can do this myself."

"But I should come with you."

"No. I don't want you there." I signalled to Mia, who was just sitting back down. "Will *you* come?"

Her eyebrows lifted in surprise, then she quickly gathered up her purse and moved past our mother.

❦

The nurse took me to a locker and handed me a green john-
nie shirt. She told me to wait for the doctor in examination
room number six, and warned me that he was slightly behind
schedule, so it could be a half hour, or more, before we got started.

Got started. That seemed, to me, a grim turn of phrase, considering that we were about to bring my short-lived pregnancy to
an end.

I felt dizzy as I climbed onto the crinkly paper on the table.
I glanced at the shiny stirrups and imagined placing my heels in
them. How long would it take? How much pain would there be?

I laid my hand on my stomach where my baby was. He, or
she, was alive inside me and growing. Mom kept telling me 'it'
was no bigger than a walnut, but that didn't make any difference
to me. Not in that moment while I waited for the doctor to arrive.

"You still look like crap," Mia said.

"I don't feel so good," I replied, hopping off the table to stand
on my feet.

"Are you going to be sick again?"

All at once, a vivid image of this baby invaded my consciousness, and I could see her as a little girl, five years old and laughing.
With red hair just like mine. The sound of her laughter was as real
in my mind as any flesh-and-blood human being standing before

me, and her joy was contagious. I experienced an immense infusion of love, as if someone had pumped it into my veins, and I knew at once that I had to leave that room.

"I can't do it," I said to Mia. "I have to have this baby. I don't know what I'm going to do yet, but if I have to put her up for adoption, then that's what I'll do."

My sister didn't question my decision or ask what had changed my mind. She simply nodded – as if she'd already known it would come to this – and rose to her feet.

"Let's get out of here," she said.

I couldn't reach the door fast enough.

When Mia and I pushed through the doors to the waiting area, my mother turned pale as a sheet. She lowered her novel and frowned at me.

"Are you finished already?"

"Yes, I'm finished," I replied, not stopping to explain.

Feeling the curious stares of two other pregnant women in the room, I locked eyes with one of them. She smiled at me, as if she knew I was like her...that I, too, had a tiny, special life growing inside of me, and wasn't it wonderful?

You're doing the right thing, a voice whispered inside my head. Was this my conscience? My higher self? Or was I reading that woman's thoughts? Could pregnant women communicate through telepathy? Was there some sort of magic at work here? Or was I going mad?

I walked out of the hospital without waiting for my mother, who learned from Mia that I had changed my mind. They stayed to explain my decision to the nurse at the desk, while I waited by the locked car in the sunny parking lot.

Mia later told me everything she had said to Mom, and I will never forget what she did for me that day, and how she spared me the ordeal of fighting for what I wanted and needed.

Mia told our mother in no uncertain terms that if she or Dad questioned or criticized my decision, they would lose me forever and never know their future grandchildren.

She was my buffer that day, my protector, and my friend.

When Mom arrived at the car and unlocked it, she said, "Well, I suppose we're going to have to come up with a new plan."

I climbed into the back seat with no idea what that plan would be. All I knew was that I needed to see Glenn.

I rode my bike to the school as soon as we got home. Basketball practice was over, but the coach had the team gathered on the bench for a pep talk.

As soon as they finished, Glenn spotted me, picked up his gear, and jogged to the door where I stood waiting. His hair was tousled and damp with perspiration, and his white cotton T-shirt clung wetly to his skin.

"I didn't expect to see you here," he said. "Are you okay?"

"I'm fine," I replied, and immediately burst into a clumsy mixture of laughter and tears.

"What happened?" he asked, confused by my response.

"I couldn't do it," I told him. I was crying more than laughing, but they were happy tears, except that I was shaking all over, terrified to imagine what our future held. "Dad's going to be so angry when he finds out. I don't know what he's going to do. What if he was serious about moving away? I can't do this without you."

Glenn dropped his bag and pulled me into his arms. He smelled of clean, fresh sweat, and when I pressed my lips to his cheek, I tasted salt.

"Everything's going to be okay," he whispered.

"Are you mad at me?"

I wondered if he might have preferred for me to go through with the abortion.

He held me at arm's length and looked into my eyes. "Mad? Never. I just wish I could have been there with you, and I'm sorry I let your parents pressure us. Deep down I knew it wasn't right. I knew you'd regret it."

"Yes, I would have, but now I don't know what we're going to do."

"We'll get through it," he said. "I promise. I still want to marry you."

"Are you sure?"

He took my face in his hands and kissed me hard. "I've never been more sure of anything in my life."

And on that day, I believed him.

I wish I could tell you that we were married a few weeks later and lived happily ever after, but fate was not so kind.

First of all, my father refused to give us permission to marry. He told us that we had to be eighteen. Years later I learned that if you're pregnant, the parental consent requirement can be waived. Maybe I was naïve, but it didn't occur to me to doubt what my father told us about the law.

Dad wanted me to go live with his sister in Boston for the duration of my pregnancy and give birth there – so that no one would ever know of my disgrace. He also wanted me to put the baby up for adoption. I couldn't agree to that – I still wasn't sure – but we did reach a compromise. I promised to consider his wishes, and when I began to show, I genuinely believed it was the best option.

I was trying to be selfless, you see. I wanted to put the baby's needs before my own, and wouldn't it be better for a child to be raised by parents who at least had a high school diploma?

Sometimes I fantasized about my baby being adopted into one of the wealthy families in town – the ones whose kids went to Ivy League colleges. Those families owned yachts and spent their summers up in Nova Scotia, where they won sailing trophies during Chester Race Week. What I wouldn't give for my child to have all the things I would never have.

Money wasn't everything, of course, and I knew that. There were plenty of responsible middle-class couples in the world that couldn't have children of their own. Maybe this was meant to be. Maybe it was why I was put here on this earth – to provide this gift to a woman who desperately wanted a child and deserved happiness. Was it possible that I was meant to connect with her?

These were questions I often pondered. I wondered why this was happening to me. There had to be a reason, surely. There had to be some sort of logic to this unexpected bomb that had exploded in my life. A purpose to the things I didn't ask for, or want.

Don't misunderstand me. I wanted my baby, more than anything in the world. I bought lottery tickets each week, hoping I would win the jackpot, and all my problems would be solved. I could buy a quaint little house with a white picket fence, and Glenn wouldn't have to work at the grocery store to support us. He could go to college, and when he graduated and our child started kindergarten, I would take my turn with higher education.

I imagine you are shaking your head. I can hardly blame you. I've always been a dreamer, wanting the impossible. Every night I looked up at the stars and wished for a good life for my baby. I didn't know what that life might entail. I was flexible in that area. I just wanted her to be happy and to know that she was loved and would have everything I wanted for her.

If only the future could have been so perfect.

When my father refused to give consent for us to marry, I believe he was clinging to the hope that I would eventually see reason and agree to put the baby up for adoption, and things would go back to the way they were.

I wanted to keep all options open, so I struck a deal with him. If I lived with his sister during my pregnancy, he would give us permission to get married after the child was born – no matter what I decided about the adoption. To my surprise he agreed to that proposal.

So I was sent to Boston for my 'confinement' as Glenn referred to it, because it all seemed so medieval.

To be honest, I wasn't sorry to leave Bar Harbor when I began to show. I didn't relish the idea of being at the center of a small town scandal and becoming fodder for all the voracious gossips.

So at least one decision was made: We were all going to keep it secret until the baby was born.

"I don't want this," Glenn said to me the night before I left.

He had come over to help me pack and say good-bye. He promised to visit, of course, but not often because he was saving every penny he earned for a deposit on a small apartment, just in case we found ourselves signing a marriage certificate in six months' time.

I zipped up my suitcase and sat down beside him on the edge of my bed. "I don't want it either," I said, "but it'll be worth it in the end if Dad lets us get married."

"How do you know we can trust him? What if he still refuses, even after you do what he asks?"

I laid my hand on Glenn's knee and shrugged lightheartedly. "Then we'll move in together. He can't stop me from doing that, and I suspect he'd rather see me legally wed than living in sin."

Cradling my chin in his hand, Glenn leaned close and kissed me. His lips were soft and warm and my body melted into his as my heart swelled with the love I felt for him. At the same time, I was in agony, for I didn't know how I was going to live without him for the next six months.

I wrapped my arms around his neck. "I hate this."

"Me too." He eased me onto my back and stroked my hair as he leaned over me. "I never imagined I could love someone like I love you. And I will love you until the day I die."

"Me, too."

His lips touched mine and we clung to each other on my bed. Then the sound of my father's footsteps tramping up the stairs forced us to sit up and let go of each other.

Five months later

Just like that woman I had seen in the hospital many months ago, I was, by now, as big as a barn, and had a habit of rubbing my hand over my belly in a soothing manner. I even talked to my belly. We had intelligent conversations about all sorts of things.

Maybe it was because I was alone in Boston with only my aunt as a roommate. I attended the local high school, but mostly kept to myself. It wasn't difficult, because everyone knew I was 'the pregnant girl from away,' who would leave at the end of the year.

You don't know how grateful I am, today, that there was no Facebook back then.

I can at least report that I grew very close to my aunt. Her name was Angela, and she was my father's youngest sister. She was single and gorgeous and worked as an account manager for an advertising firm downtown. I loved the way she dressed in classy suits with skinny skirts and high heels. She was such a modern city woman. Part of me envied her freedom and lifestyle, for I knew it was highly unlikely that I would ever achieve such success – not if I never graduated from high school, which was a very real possibility if I kept this baby. Yet, I was content with my lot. I knew this baby would be special.

Mia wrote to me often and told me to 'hang in there.' She believed that when push came to shove, Mom and Dad would do what was necessary to help Glenn and me finish school.

I wasn't so sure about that, but I remained ever hopeful.

And Glenn…I missed him so much, there were days I feared I might turn to dust and blow away on a light breeze. If not for his letters, which arrived dependably each day – they were hand-written; we didn't have email yet – I might have packed it in and returned home before my due date. His words of love and encouragement kept me from jumping onto the next train.

I read those letters so many times, I could have recited them all by memory. I still have them today. They are locked away in a small cedar box at the back of my closet, and every once in awhile I dig them out. I like to remember those days of young love. We were so passionate and full of hope for the future.

I also have Mia's letters, but I don't often read them. It's too painful, especially the last one, where she wrote to tell me that she had a wonderful surprise for me.

Mia's surprise turned out to be the sound of her knocking on Angela's door late one Saturday morning, three weeks before my due date.

"What are you doing here?" I squealed with delight as I pulled her into the apartment and hugged the daylights out of her.

She looked gorgeous as usual, and had a new spiral perm, a flashy red purse, and the cutest pair of black and white high top sneakers.

"I wanted to surprise you," she replied, "and bring you this." She held up a small black bag.

"What is it?" I took it from her, peered inside, and laughed out loud. "It's Bubba!"

My sister had brought the teddy bear I hugged and loved almost my entire life. He was freshly laundered and wore a cute new dress. Forget that he was a male bear. Mia loved skirts.

"I thought you might like to give him to your little one, because he's full of love, remember?"

Of course I remembered. Mom made Bubba with a Butterick pattern when I was born, and when I was six years old, I sewed a tiny felt heart, stuffed it with cotton, and she helped me rip apart the seam at his side to insert it into his chest.

I hugged Bubba tight. "It's perfect, Mia. I'm so glad you thought of it. Well, don't just stand there. Come in. Are you hungry? I'm hungry all the time. Did you eat on the train?"

"I had a sandwich," she said. "Where's Angela?"

"At work."

"On a Saturday?"

"Yeah. She has a big presentation on Monday. Such is the life of a busy career woman."

Mia set her suitcase down in the hallway and followed me into the living room.

Angela lived in a two-bedroom apartment with somewhat dingy wall-to-wall carpeting, a tiny kitchen, but a spectacular view of the city. She lived on the sixteenth floor of a highrise, which meant the sunsets were spectacular. Later, I would miss those sunsets, after I moved home.

"How are Mom and Dad?" I asked, setting the kettle on the stove to make tea.

Mia sat down at the table and shrugged out of her jacket. "They're fine. Everything's as normal as can be, but Mom told me to give you this." She reached into her purse and withdrew an envelope, which she slid across the table.

I moved closer to pick it up. It was a business-sized envelope with no name or address written on the outside. It was not a greeting card, as I might have expected.

I broke the seal and found one hundred dollars cash inside. "What's this for?"

"For whatever you might need," Mia replied. "She didn't mention it to Dad. She handed it to me very discreetly when she drove me to the train station this morning."

"Tell her thank you," I said. I slipped it into my purse, which hung on the back of a kitchen chair. Then I went to check to make sure the kettle was heating up.

"How long can you stay?" I asked Mia.

"Just until tomorrow night. I have to get back for work on Monday."

I felt a thickness in my throat and wanted nothing more than to pack my things and return home with her on the train, sleep in my own bed, see my friends, and be with Glenn.

Only three more weeks, I told myself. *Then I can go home.*

Little did I know that it would happen sooner than that, and when I returned to Bar Harbor, life would never be the same again.

C H A P T E R

Twenty-six

That night, Angela took us to her favorite pizza place. I ate three large slices, knowing full well that I would pay for it later with a spell of heartburn that would keep me up most of the night.

It was not heartburn that woke me at 5:00 in the morning, however. I sat up when my bedroom door creaked open and Angela appeared as a silhouette against the harsh light from the hallway.

Mia, who slept on a foam mattress on the floor beside me, sat up as well. We squinted at Angela. She wore a white silk, knee-length nightgown, and stood in silence like a phantom, breathing heavily as if she had just run a marathon. I wondered if she was sleepwalking.

"What's going on?" Mia asked.

Angela took an unsteady step forward, then sank to her knees. I knew immediately that something was wrong and flung the covers off to leap out of bed. I rushed to her side and knelt down. "What's wrong, Angela?"

She laid a hand on her chest. "I can't breathe. I think I'm having a heart attack."

Mia leaped to her feet. "Oh, my God. Should we call an ambulance?" she asked me.

"Yes." I pointed to the door. "Go call 911. Tell them what's happening, give them our address, and tell them we're on the sixteenth floor. We'll have to buzz them in when they arrive."

Mia ran out while I remained with Angela. "Try and stay calm," I said, helping her to lie down on the floor, not knowing if that was the right thing to do or not. "You're going to be fine. The ambulance will be here soon."

She nodded at me, but I saw the panic in her eyes. She was pasty gray and perspiring. She gripped my hand tightly. Her palm was clammy.

"Everything's going to be fine," I said, and gently rubbed her hair off her face. "Maybe it's just a bad reaction to the pizza."

She nodded again, but we both knew it was more than that. She squeezed my hand and held it to her heart. "Thank you, Kate. I'm so sorry. I'm supposed to be taking care of *you*."

"You *are* taking care of me," I said. "I don't know what I would have done without you these past few months."

She winced with pain and shut her eyes. I felt a rush of fear. "Are you okay?" I asked. "Can I do anything?"

"Just stay with me," she managed to say.

I didn't understand how this could be happening. Angela was young, fit, and vibrant. She went to yoga class three times a week and had never mentioned anything about a heart condition.

"Has this ever happened to you before?" I asked.

"No, never."

Mia ran back into the room. "The ambulance is on its way."

W hen the paramedics wheeled the gurney into Angela's apartment, I wanted to bow at their feet and kiss their boots. Everything about them put me at ease. They wore uniforms like police officers, and wasted no time reaching Angela. They knelt on either side of her and calmly began asking questions about her symptoms.

"What's your name?" the dark-haired one asked.

"Angela Worthington."

"My name is Scott, and I'm a paramedic. This is John. Can you tell me what's wrong?"

Angela described her chest pains, her difficulty breathing, and a pain in her left arm that she had not mentioned to Mia or me.

"Have you ever had pain like this before?" Scott asked.

"No, never."

"How long has it been going on? Did it start suddenly or creep up on you?"

"The pain woke me about an hour ago."

While Scott took Angela's pulse, John said, "I'm going to put this blood pressure cup on your arm, Angela, and then I'm going to attach some EKG leads to your chest so we can find out what's going on."

Angela nodded while Mia and I stood out of the way, watching.

I am quite sure that was the moment that sealed my fate, though I didn't realize it at the time. I made no conscious decision that I wanted to be a paramedic. I couldn't even see past the fact that I was eight months pregnant and might never finish high school. All I knew was that I worshipped those EMTs, and I was immensely grateful for their skills.

Scott asked, "Can you scale the pain from one to ten? If ten is excruciating——"

"Seven," Angela said.

The two paramedics locked eyes briefly, then continued their assessment.

"Any family history?" Scott asked.

"My uncle had a triple bypass four years ago. He was fifty-eight."

"How old are you?"

"Thirty-two."

"Are you on any medications? Do you smoke?"

"No."

"Are you on any other drugs? Cocaine, uppers, downers, speed, herbal medications?"

"No."

"Are you *sure?*" Scott firmly asked. "We need to know everything, Angela, otherwise we can't help you."

I knew they doubted her denial because she was so young. It hardly seemed possible that she could be at risk for a heart attack.

"She's not on drugs," I answered in her defense.

John, the stocky one, turned his head and looked up at me, as if for the first time. His gaze lingered on my belly for a few seconds, then he went back to work on Angela. He started an IV tube and put an oxygen mask on her.

"It looks like she has ST elevations in lead two," John said.

Scott called the hospital. "We've got a thirty-two-year-old woman with a possible MI. Pain started an hour ago, radiating into the left arm. She's diaphoretic. Some family history." He paused. "No, it was an uncle. No drugs, no other risk factors." Another pause. "Yeah, we have her on O2. Would like permission to give aspirin and nitroglycerin."

Scott nodded and snapped his fingers at John, who briefly removed the oxygen mask to slip a pill under Angela's tongue.

Suddenly, I felt a pain in my lower abdomen and clutched my stomach. "Oh no," I said, looking down at the floor.

Scott hung up and said to Angela, "We're going to take you to the hospital now." Then he approached me. "Are you okay?"

"No," I replied. "I think my water just broke."

Mia gripped my shoulder. "Oh, my God. Does this mean you're going into labor?"

"Where are your parents?" Scott asked, still blessedly calm in the midst of all this.

"They live in Bar Harbor," I replied. "Angela is my aunt. I've been staying with her for a while. This is my sister."

Scott studied Mia's panic-stricken face. "Then I think you should both come with us to the hospital. You can ride in the ambulance." He turned to help John lift Angela onto the gurney. "What's your name?" he asked me.

"Kate."

"Nice to meet you, Kate. Why don't you go pack a few things, but hurry up. You have exactly one minute and then we're out of here."

Twenty-eight

"How is she doing?" I asked Scott as the ambulance picked up speed.

John was at the wheel. He had turned on the siren as soon as we were underway.

"Why don't we ask her?" Scott said. "How are you feeling, Angela?"

She lay on the gurney, still wearing the oxygen mask, and gave a thumbs up.

"Everything's going to be fine," Scott said. "There's hardly any traffic, so we should reach the hospital in about ten minutes. How about you, Kate?" he said to me. "Are you feeling any contractions?"

I shook my head. "No, nothing after that first time when my water broke. Is this normal?"

"It's nothing to be concerned about," he replied. "They'll take good care of you."

By 'they,' he meant the doctors and nurses on the obstetrical floor at the hospital.

I wasn't due for three weeks, and I wondered if my premature labor had been brought on by the stress of Angela's heart attack.

"How old are you, anyway, if you don't mind my asking?"

Scott constantly amazed me by how he could carry on a conversation while checking an IV or taking Angela's blood pressure.

"I'm sixteen," I replied.

"Is that why you're not living with your parents?"

"Yeah," I said, "but this is only temporary until the baby is born. They didn't kick me out or anything like that, but we live in a small town and felt it would be better this way."

"Are you putting the baby up for adoption?"

"Why would you assume that?" I asked, wanting to hear Scott's opinion on the matter, because I was still undecided about whether or not I should keep the baby.

Scott shrugged non-committedly. "I just figured that must be the case if you're having the baby here and not at home. Otherwise, why keep it a secret, if everyone's going to know anyway?"

It was a reasonable deduction, and just when I was about to tell him that I was leaning toward keeping my baby, Mia said, "I think you should keep it. It's the right thing. I have a feeling about this baby. She's going to be special."

"*She?* What makes you think it's a girl?"

She shrugged. "I don't know. I just have this funny feeling. Either way, it doesn't matter. I promise to help you. We'll convince Mom and Dad together."

I had never loved her more than I did in that moment.

Then suddenly, John hollered, "*Shit!*"

He slammed on the brakes.

It all happened very quickly after that. Mia and I tumbled over each other on the bench, then a sudden jarring impact shattered the quiet morning as the ambulance was rammed at a ninety-degree angle by what I later learned was a mid-sized moving truck.

The sound of crunching metal and smashing glass was explosive in my ears. Mia slammed into me. I felt the crack of her skull against mine and the tangle of her flailing limbs as she rolled over me.

When John first hit the brakes, Angela's gurney shot forward against the driver's compartment like a projectile, then she spun like a log on water as we flipped over sideways. Three times apparently. I have no memory of that. The last thing I remember is the concern I felt at the terrible pain in my belly when I was flung violently into a shelf of medical supplies.

CHAPTER

Twenty-nine

The accident occurred at 5:58 in the morning. I was later told that on the evening news, it was reported that the driver of the moving truck had been up all night helping his girlfriend clear out of her apartment.

He was drunk, and he died instantly when he flew through the windshield.

I woke twelve days later to the monotonous beep of a heart monitor. When I was finally able to grasp that this was not a normal awakening, I struggled to open my eyes, but my body didn't seem able to respond to my wishes. I was confused by this, but it was nothing compared to the throbbing pain in my head and a slow realization…

I was lying in a hospital bed, because I had been injured in an ambulance accident.

"Kate? Can you hear me? I think she's awake. Lester, go and get someone."

Though my mind was in a fog and the pain in my head made it difficult to think clearly, I could at least recognize my mother's voice. I then became cognizant of the fact that my left arm was in a cast.

All at once, memories rushed at me like blinding flashes of light.

I was riding in the ambulance. There was a loud crash. I saw Angela's gurney fly through the air.

With growing panic, I began to breathe heavily. "My baby... Is my baby okay?"

My father hurried into the room with a nurse. She checked my vitals. I couldn't understand why no one would answer my question.

"My baby..." I said. "Mia...*Where's Mia?*"

"Try to stay calm," Dad said. "We need to make sure you're okay."

"Everything looks good," the nurse told him. "I'm going to call the doctor."

My mother began to weep.

I could barely find the strength to move, but somehow I managed to slide my hand up onto my belly.

It was *flat*.

My father leaned over the bed. "I'm sorry, Kate," he said. "It was a very bad accident. No one survived but you. You're lucky to be alive."

But I didn't feel lucky at all. I felt as if my father had just pushed me off the roof of a tall city skyscraper. I was plummeting fast, trapped in some sort of horrific dimension of disbelief. I thought I might be dreaming. It couldn't be true. Yet I knew it was, because my stomach was flat and there was a scar, low on my abdomen, which meant my womb was empty. I was no longer carrying a child inside of me. My body had been jostled about violently and I was ravaged and broken.

My baby was dead.

And Mia, Angela...All dead.

Yet here I was. *Alive.*

The rescue team had called it a miracle, because both para-medics died on the scene, as did as Angela, Mia, and my unborn child.

I was the only survivor.

But why me?

Into the Future

February 17, 2007

Do you remember the woman from the frozen lake? The one who had no vitals when we transported her to the hospital? Her name was Sophie. She had been dead for more than forty minutes before they revived her, and I couldn't seem to get her out of my head.

"Did that woman from the lake ever come out of her coma?" I asked Bill as we headed out on a call.

"I asked about her yesterday," he replied. "They said she still hasn't woken up. She'll probably be a vegetable."

I gazed out the window as we sped past a playground. "Slow down. There are kids around here."

"You're always telling me to slow down, but can I remind you that this is an emergency vehicle? We're *supposed* to speed."

"You know how I feel about that," I replied.

Bill and I had been partners for six months before I told him what happened to me almost twenty years earlier. Like most people, he was surprised I decided to become a paramedic after something like that. I've often wondered about that myself, and I have no answer to give, except to say that this is what I was born to do.

We raced through an intersection and nearly collided with two cop cars that fishtailed around the corner ahead of us. I instinctively gripped the door handle to hang on.

⤳

When we arrived at the scene – which was an apartment building parking lot in a rough section of town – the cops were clearing people out of the way. Bill and I hurried to get the stretcher out and wheeled it toward a man who was lying face down on the pavement next to a rusted-out white van.

A woman was on her knees beside him, screaming hysterically. "Hurry!" she shouted at us. "He's shot!"

One of the cops helped pull her to her feet. "Move back, ma'am. You have to give them some room."

I knelt down and saw a blood stain at the man's right shoulder blade. "Turn him over," I said to Bill.

We rolled the victim onto his back. He looked to be in his mid-fifties, with long, thinning hair and a beard. There was another stain of blood on his chest. "The entry wound is here," I said. I searched for a pulse. My gaze met Bill's and I nodded. "He's alive. Let's get him on the stretcher."

Bill helped me lift him, and as soon as we started wheeling the victim toward the ambulance, another van pulled into the lot and a news team spilled out. The cameraman started filming us, while a female reporter plugged in a microphone and began interviewing witnesses.

By that time, we had reached the ambulance and were sliding the stretcher into the back. I got in, and Bill shut the doors behind us. Seconds later Bill was back in the driver's seat and we took off for the hospital, with lights flashing and siren blaring.

This was my life now, and chaos felt as natural to me as breathing.

❧

A full trauma team was waiting for us when we arrived. I quickly gave my report to the doctors as we wheeled the victim inside, explaining that the bullet had entered the right lateral chest and gone straight through. I stepped back when we reached the trauma room.

A half hour later, after I finished filing my report, my shift ended. I was about to head home, but felt strangely compelled to take the elevator up to the seventh floor and ask about the woman from the lake, who I couldn't seem to get out of my head.

"How's she doing?" I asked at the nurses' station. "Any improvement?"

"Afraid not," the male clerk replied. "She's had lots of visitors, though. There's a guy who comes and plays guitar for her every night. Nice family."

I peered down the hall. "What room is she in?"

"Second on the left. I think her sister's in there now if you want to say hello. I'm sure she'd like to talk to you, since you're the one who brought her sister back from the dead."

"It wasn't really me," I clarified. "It was the defibrillator that brought her back. I just warmed her up."

The clerk gave me a look as if to suggest I was being too modest, then gestured for me to go and pay a visit.

I don't know why I was so uneasy about it. I suppose I didn't want to face the woman's sister, who might want to ask me questions about what happened – or thank me, when I had just been doing my job.

Besides, what was there to be thankful for? Life could be total shit sometimes. The woman had been down for at least forty minutes. Odds that she would ever recover, and live a normal life, were slim to nil.

Nevertheless, as if by some irresistible force, I was drawn to that room.

I knocked softly on the open door. When no one responded, I ventured inside to find the room vacant – except for the woman lying comatose on the bed.

The heart monitor beeped a steady rhythm. Vases of flowers covered every available surface, and magazines were spread out on the windowsill. My gaze remained fixed on the woman, however, as I moved closer to where she lay.

She looked far more alive than she had in the back of my ambulance, though she wasn't exactly radiant at the moment. She was flat on her back with her hands folded across her abdomen, as if she were laid out for a funeral wake. Her lips were dry and cracked. Her complexion was the color of ash.

I leaned over her and studied her face. "What a fighter you must be," I softly said, "but really, what's the point?"

She offered no reply.

"Are you even in there?" I asked. "Can you hear me?"

"I think she's in there," a voice said from the doorway, and I jumped.

Swinging around, I locked eyes with a slender blonde-haired woman who looked to be about my age. "I'm sorry," I replied, mortified by the questions I had just asked. "I didn't mean to intrude."

She glanced down at my uniform. "It's fine. You must be the paramedic."

I nodded, and she walked toward me. "I'm Jen, Sophie's sister."

"It's nice to meet you." We shook hands, and an awkward silence descended upon the room. "I'm sorry about what happened to her," I said. "The roads were really bad that night."

Jen backed up to lean against the windowsill. "That's what they tell me. But listen...thanks for what you did. For bringing her back. We're very grateful."

Again, I waved a dismissive hand through the air. "All I did was warm her up in the ambulance. It was the trauma team that brought her back, here at the hospital. They're the ones you should thank."

Jen shrugged, as if it was all the same to her. "What do you think her chances are?" she asked me.

"I honestly can't say," I replied, not wanting to crush this woman's hopes, even though I had very little faith of my own that Sophie would ever return to the world of the living, much less to the woman she once was, for I had quit believing in miracles a long time ago. "Every case is different."

"That's what the doctors tell me," Jen said, "but it's hard, you know."

I glanced at Sophie and remembered exactly how it felt to wake up in a bed just like this one, then hear the news that my baby was dead. And my sister. And my aunt.

Was there any life left inside of *me*? I wondered. Any hope? Sometimes I felt like a crazy person. I wanted to run screaming down the street, calling out for Mia and my baby.

Sometimes I woke from a dream where I heard my child's laughter, just as I had in the hospital that day when I chose not to have the abortion. I wanted so badly to go to her.

Did that mean I wanted to die? That I wanted to go to heaven to be with her?

There were times when the answer was yes. Glenn had certainly given up on living. Once he said, 'I'd be better off dead. I just hope that when it happens, our daughter will be there at the pearly gates to greet me.'

It had become my task these days to try and prevent the loss of Glenn, too. Maybe that's why I became a paramedic. Maybe I knew I would one day need these skills to save his life. I certainly didn't want to lose anyone else that I loved.

I was always looking for the reason behind things. The purpose.

Why, this? Or why, that?

It had been almost twenty years since my accident, but I was still haunted by it – by all that I had lost that night. What was the purpose of that? Of all the suffering? Had I done something to deserve it? Or was it some sort of test?

"Yes, I know." I quickly shook the memories away and faced Jen. "I really should get going. My husband's waiting for me at home. It was nice to meet you. I'm sorry about your sister. I hope she'll be okay."

Jen appeared startled by my sudden compulsion to leave, but I just couldn't stay in that room any longer. It was too close to death.

When I arrived home, it was the usual scene. All the lights were off, but the television was on.

I set down my purse and keys and walked through the kitchen. Glenn was passed out on the sofa with an empty bottle of vodka on the floor beside him. I saw the disturbing telltale signs of a cocaine binge – the hand mirror on the coffee table, the straw, and the credit card.

God…!

A sudden violent rage rose up within me. Why was Glenn doing this? I understood that life hadn't been easy on either of us. We got married too young, hoping to replace the child we lost and find happiness again. But that wasn't in the cards. Not for us. I'd had a string of miscarriages. My mother was gone now, and we didn't even speak to my father. We had no family to lean on. There was nothing but grief.

Yet somehow, I managed to cope. Managed to go on living.

Tonight I saw a woman who had fought hard enough to come back from the dead, and she was still fighting to live.

Meanwhile my husband was slowly killing himself, and ruining us financially in the process, for he had been fired from his job three weeks ago, and there was nothing left of our savings. A hot and bitter anger swept through me.

I couldn't take it anymore. I couldn't go on enabling his addictions. It was time to make a change, and I vowed I would not accept any more false promises. Tomorrow I would ask him – one last time – to enter rehab. If he refused, I would tell him to leave. I would cancel all our credit cards, change the locks on the house, and consult a lawyer.

That night, I didn't cover Glenn with a blanket. I didn't care about him, or anything. I left him there in the dark, and went straight to bed.

It was a decision I would later regret.

Another Life

Ryan Hamilton

I've often wondered why bad things happen to good people. Is it simply a matter of luck and timing? Or are certain people born under a shining star that emits magic fairy dust of good fortune? Maybe some folks have superstars for guardian angels, while others get stuck with slackers. It's simply the luck of the draw. Or unluckiness...

My name is Ryan Hamilton and I should begin by explaining that I am a man of science. I hold a bachelor's degree in neuroscience, which I received with high honors. I also hold a medical degree. I have been an emergency medicine doctor for twenty-two years and I've saved many lives. Should I therefore know more than the average person about life and death, and the endurance of the human spirit? I wish I could say yes, but unfortunately science can only answer so many questions – those that can be tested and proven.

But what about all the magic that surrounds us on a daily basis? What about fate and destiny and crazy, impossible good luck?

We've all witnessed miracles of some kind or another in our lives. I'm sure you've experienced something that makes you wonder about the existence of a higher power? Cosmic forces? The electrical energy of life? Or God?

I don't know if God exists, but I do know one thing.

There is much in our world that can't be explained. Certain events defy reason or possibility. What seems unbelievable can occur before our very eyes and leave us speechless with awe.

For this reason, I feel compelled to tell you my story, because I will continue to be awed by what I witnessed until I draw my last breath.

CHAPTER

Thirty-three

Ↄↄ

I'm sure, if you're like most people, you sometimes wince when
you remember certain stupid things you did in your youth.
Things you're not proud of, things you would never do today,
knowing what you know now. In fact, you probably consider
yourself lucky to have gotten away with those bad decisions,
but you're thankful you learned something in the process. For
me, those lessons came at a very high price one fateful night in
Ontario.

"Pass me another beer," John said as he glanced over his
shoulder at me in the car.

We were seventeen years old. I was seated in the back seat,
slouched low with the cooler at my feet.

John was in the front passenger seat, and his girlfriend Lisa
was driving. We were on our way to a party we'd gotten wind of
earlier that day, way out in the country.

Lisa was our designated driver, but that didn't count for
much. When I handed the beer to John, he broke the seal on the
can and passed it to Lisa, who guzzled half of it before handing
it back.

"Ahh!" she said in a great exhale. "That's good, but now I
need to burp." She fisted her chest, opened her mouth wide, and
belched like a trucker.

"That's my girl," John said, leaning close to kiss her neck. She smiled and turned to kiss him on the mouth, then swerved alarmingly when she returned her attention to the road.

Luckily we were in the middle of nowhere, so there was no oncoming traffic. It was pitch dark and we were speeding along a flat, straight country road with cornfields on either side of us.

I was so drunk I could barely focus on the yellow lines illuminated by the headlights, so I leaned my head against the side window, folded my arms across my chest, and closed my eyes.

I'll be the first to admit that I was an idiot when I was seventeen – a quintessential angry young man but I was also a product of my environment. Financially speaking, I came from a world of privilege. My father was a corporate attorney and my mother was a successful real estate agent. I am an only child because they waited a long time to start a family. First, they wanted to get all their social ducks in a row – to be in the right house, the right neighborhood. Since my mother was the one who would sacrifice the most in terms of her career, she put it off for as long as possible. She was thirty-seven years old and CEO of a multi-million-dollar real estate firm when she gave birth to me.

She took a three-month maternity leave, but worked from home the entire time, then hired a live-in nanny to care for me, cook the meals, and keep the house tidy. Basically, my mother had what she said all working women needed – a wife to keep the home fires burning.

Unfortunately, when I was two years old, the home fires burned a little too hotly when my father began sleeping with the twenty-one-year-old nanny. A messy divorce followed, and my father lost everything. Not only did my mother get the summer lake house in the Muskokas and the downtown penthouse apartment, she also kept the Mercedes and received full custody of me.

My father received limited visitation rights – I don't think he fought hard for anything more – and a year later, the nanny left him for a younger man. My father lived alone in a Queen Street flat for about six months. Then he put a pistol in his mouth one night after eating a frozen pizza for dinner. When I was older, I was told he had been charged with embezzlement that day.

What followed was a string of nannies who all left me eventually, to move on to other things. My mother was a workaholic who viewed me as another material asset to invest in, so I think it's reasonable to conclude that I had some issues with abandonment.

When I was twelve years old, my mother decided that a twenty-four-hour, live-in babysitter was no longer required.

"Ryan," she said, "you're perfectly capable of making your own breakfast and lunch, and getting yourself to school on time." She told me she wanted to raise a capable and independent young man who knew how to take care of himself, so Mrs. Puglisi was hired as a housemaid and cook, with instructions to keep an occasional eye on me when I was around. She was not to prepare my snacks, wash my clothes, or 'coddle' me in any way. It was time I learned how to do things on my own.

With this new independence, and a lack of any personal connection to Mrs. Puglisi or my mother, I usually went to my friends' houses after school, because their mothers worked, too – but they didn't have cranky housekeepers with eagle eyes.

I had my first beer at the age of thirteen in John's basement. My mom showed homes and properties most evenings, which meant I had far too much freedom for a thirteen-year-old. I'm still not sure if she genuinely believed in me, and trusted me to behave like a mature, responsible adult, or if she simply preferred to stick her head in the sand and let me do as I pleased.

At fourteen, John and I began experimenting with marijuana, and he was expelled from school for bringing hashish brownies for the entire homeroom class on Valentine's Day. I knew about them, of course, but at least I had the sense not to help him bake and frost them.

We remained friends, even when he was forced to attend a different school, and though he was a terrible influence on me and got me into all sorts of trouble and dangerous situations – like what happened to us that night – it was his friendship that taught me a lesson I desperately needed to learn.

W hen I woke in the back seat of John's car, we were still driving, but now we were surrounded by thick dark forest on either side.

"Where are we?" I asked, sitting up groggily and looking around.

"We're almost there," John replied. He raised a pint of whisky to his lips, tipped it up, and chugged it.

"Give me some of that," I said, reaching out to take it as he passed it over the seat.

"*Whoohoo!*" he shouted, and cranked up the radio when ACDC came on. "We're gonna get shit-faced tonight! How do we open the sunroof?" he asked Lisa while he searched the dash for a button.

She reached up and adjusted the controls. The tinted window above us slid open with a quiet hum, and through the heavy haze of my drunkenness, I could see the stars.

John stood up on his seat and stuck his head out. "What a night! *Yeah!*"

Lisa laughed again and cranked the music even louder until I could feel the rumble of the bass inside my chest.

I felt a little queasy as I watched John struggle to find his footing on the center console between the two front seats, then

hoist himself up through the small opening. Was he going to
climb onto the roof? I couldn't seem to make sense of what he
was doing. My vision was blurred and I could barely think.

"You're nuts!" Lisa cried out with amusement. "*Oh, Jesus!*"

Considering the state I was in, it's a wonder I saw what happened because everything spun out of control so quickly.

A racoon had waddled onto the road, and Lisa swerved to
avoid him. I was tossed against the side window and John's legs
disappeared from view, as if he'd been sucked out by a tornado.

Then Lisa drove us straight into a tree.

I don't know how long I was out. It felt like only a few seconds, but when I came to, ACDC was no longer playing on the radio. It was some other band I cannot recall.

I sat forward as if waking from a dream and touched my hand to my forehead. Slowly, dizzily, I realized my face was covered in blood, which dripped from just above my left temple. I wiped the blood away from my eyes and blinked a few times to see past the blur of my confusion.

Lisa was hunched forward over the steering wheel. I tried to open the car door. My hands shook uncontrollably. Somehow I managed to flick the latch and push it open. Spilling out onto the forest floor, I fell to my hands and knees and vomited.

The next thing I remember is pressing Lisa's shoulders back to push her away from the steering wheel. Her head fell limply against the seat and she turned toward me. I thought she was looking at me, but her eyes were dead, unseeing.

Horrorstruck, I sucked in a breath. *What should I do?* I needed help, but I had no cell phone. It was 1987.

John...

I laid the flat of my hand on the roof where the tinted glass window was still open. Where was he?

Staggering weakly up the embankment and onto the road, it was difficult to make anything out in the darkness. The headlights of the car continued to shine into the forest, but John had been thrown out of the vehicle many yards back.

"John!" I shouted, but only my voice echoed back to me in the clear, starlit night. Crickets chirped noisily while music from the car radio grew more distant as I trudged with heavy feet along the pavement. "John!"

Then I spotted something – a heap at the side of the road, just ahead.

I began to jog. My heart beat thunderously in my chest. "John!"

Terrified that he would be dead like Lisa, I dropped to my knees beside him. It was dark, but my eyes had adjusted to the moonlight's bluish glow, and I was able to make out his face.

His eyes were wide open. A trail of blood from his ear formed a thick black puddle, like chocolate syrup, on the pavement. Those wide, terrorized eyes shifted to meet mine. His lips moved.

"Ub...ub...ub..."

He stared at me, desperate and afraid. I could barely breathe. I was now completely sober, all my senses buzzing with awareness.

"Don't worry," I said, laying my hand on his shoulder and glancing down at his mangled body, his legs and torso twisted grotesquely.

"Ub...ub...ub..."

I will never forget the eerie sight of his lips moving, and the faint, husky sound of his voice in the night.

In that moment, twin headlight beams appeared from around the bend, and I rose to my feet. I waved my arms frantically over my head and moved quickly to the center of the road.

CHAPTER

Thirty-six

It seemed to take forever for the cops and paramedics to arrive. When at last they put John on the stretcher, his eyes were still wide open, but he was able to answer their questions by blinking once for yes, twice for no. They took us together in the back of the ambulance. I was able to sit on the bench while John was strapped in with a neck brace.

"Ub…ub…ub…" It was all he could say, and he kept uttering that sound over and over. What did it mean? Was he asking for something? Trying to tell us something?

"Just try to relax," the paramedic said as he checked John's pulse. "You're in good hands. We're taking you to North York General Hospital." He looked over at me. "What's your name?"

"Ryan," I said. "Ryan Hamilton."

"Do you know his parents? They'll probably want to talk to you."

"Yeah," I replied. "I know his parents."

His father would be disappointed he wouldn't be able to smack John around for this. It's how he usually dealt with such things.

None of us had been wearing seatbelts. Lisa was pronounced dead at the scene and John survived. Barely. He was paralyzed from the neck down and suffered substantial brain damage caused by a fractured skull and an epidural hematoma, which was a bleed in the brain. The bleed had caused blown pupils, explaining the strange eyes I saw.

He had a fractured C4 that severed his spinal cord. One level higher, he wouldn't have survived more than a few minutes, for it would have paralyzed his diaphragm. His brain injury improved, which may not have been a good thing, because he was stuck in a wheelchair for the rest of his life and grew very bitter. I tried to visit several times but he wouldn't see any of us.

It wasn't easy to lose my best friend, and I can't possibly say that anything good came of it – not for John. It still pains me deeply to think of his misery.

~~6~~

Two years later, I graduated from high school at the top of my class, which shocked all my teachers and my disinterested mother, who had no idea I was performing so well. She had never asked. But after the accident, something clicked inside of me and I began to question my existence, and my good luck, for I had emerged from a fatal accident with only a few scratches.

Why had I survived? Why me? Was there some greater purpose I was meant to discover or achieve?

Everything changed for me overnight. I finally realized how fragile and precious life was. I quit drinking and partying. I took an interest in school – science in particular – and eventually in human anatomy and the workings of that complex organ inside our heads. The more I learned, the more magic I saw in the world, for how could such a wonder of nature – the brain – ever come to exist? Everything I learned was based on science, yet my own survival that night – and further events that were about to occur in my life – never ceased to amaze me. Everyday still seems like a miracle to me, with no scientific explanation whatsoever, but at least I know one thing for sure: life is a gift that should not be squandered.

~~~~

I was offered scholarships to a number of universities and chose Carleton, in Ottawa, which had a good neuroscience program. I chose not to live in residence because I wanted to live alone and focus on my studies. It paid off later when I was offered spots at three different medical schools across the country. I decided to accept the offer from Dalhousie, in Nova Scotia, because I wanted to broaden my horizons and see something of the world outside of Ontario. And something about living on the Atlantic coast struck a resonating chord in me.

I completed my family medicine residency in Halifax and chose to settle on the South Shore in the small picturesque seaside community of Chester. Imagine giant pine trees, hundreds of private rocky coves to explore, and a plethora of yachts and sailboats out on the Bay on Sunday afternoons.

As far as work was concerned, I wasn't contributing anything extraordinary to neurological research, nor was I saving lives on the operating table. I chose to be a small town doctor who mostly wrote prescriptions for ear and sinus infections, helped educate patients about high cholesterol and heart disease, and covered the ER in the Bridgewater Hospital a few times a month. The most complicated procedure of an entire week might be the removal of a fishing hook from a lobsterman's finger, or the plastering of a cast on a twelve-year-old's arm after he was slammed too hard against the boards during a hockey tournament.

For the most part, it was pretty basic stuff, but then, on a regular Monday afternoon – during one of the hottest summers anyone could remember in half a century – she entered my office. And my true purpose in the world became clear.

"Honestly, I don't know what's wrong with her."
Abigail Smith – a curvy, knockout of a woman with golden hair and blue eyes – struggled to hold her daughter still on the examination table. Marissa was twenty-two months old and flailed about like a banshee, screaming her lungs out.

"She never cries like this," Abigail said. "Something is definitely wrong, but she doesn't have a fever. She keeps wincing and lifting her shoulders, like the pain is inside her head. I'm in a panic, Dr. Hamilton. You know about my husband, right? He died of a brain aneurysm not long after Marissa was born, before you came here. It was very sudden, but he complained about a headache just before. What if the same thing is happening to Marissa?"

I flicked on my otoscope to look inside Marissa's left ear. "Just hold her still for a minute. That's good. Everything looks clear here. I need to check the other one." Abigail and I switched places while Marissa continued to scream. "And brain aneurysms are rare," I said as I leaned forward to look inside. "This could be anything. A simple ear infection. *Ah.* I see the problem."

"What is it?"

I straightened and turned off my otoscope. "There's a small spider in the canal, trapped up against her ear drum."

Marissa screamed again.

Abigail's giant blue eyes blinked a few times, and her head drew back in surprise. "You're kidding me. Oh God, can you get it out? It's not going to crawl into her brain is it?"

I chuckled, mostly to help Abigail relax – though the flush in her cheeks was quite attractive and I was finding it difficult not to stare. "There's nothing to worry about. I'll have it out of there in a minute or two, but I'll need you to lay her down on her side and hold her still. Can you do that?"

"Yes, but how did it get in there?" she shouted over her daughter's shrill cries, while I went to fill a syringe with saline.

"Who knows," I replied. "It could have happened anywhere. A spider landed on my arm just the other day while I was driving. Rappelled down from the roof on a strand of web. It's nothing you did."

"How big is it?" she asked with concern.

"It's very small. Just a baby, like Marissa." I approached the table and leaned over her, and was surprised when Marissa looked me directly in the eye, and stopped crying when I spoke. "I'm going to flush some water into your ear, kiddo. Then you'll feel better, okay?"

She blinked up at me, glanced at the syringe, and nodded.

"Just lie still," I said. I gently pushed the saline into her ear canal, and the spider swam out. I grabbed hold of him with a pair of tweezers and placed him in a stainless steel bowl. "There. All gone. You can sit up now, Marissa."

Her forehead and cheekbones were blotchy from crying so hard, and she wiped her eyes with her small fist.

Abigail picked her up and held her. She turned away from me. "There, there, it's all right now. You did great, sweetheart. You were very brave."

"All gone," Marissa said, looking at me over her mother's shoulder. She reached out with her little hand, and I took hold of her fingers for a moment, smiling at her. Something inside me turned over like a stalled car engine coming to life.

"She's going to be fine," I said as Abigail faced me again. I was forced to let go of Marissa's hand.

"Thank you, Doctor Hamilton," Abigail said. "You saved the day."

Her smile was brighter than the sun.

I think I fell for both of them simultaneously that afternoon. It was love at first sight with no reasonable explanation. I had only just met Abigail. All I knew was that I was completely captivated, and I hated watching them walk out of my office. Thankfully, it would not be long before I saw them again.

A week later, I bumped into Abigail at the grocery store. We were both there to buy fresh local corn. Marissa sat cheerfully in the cart, swinging her little legs back and forth.

"Hi Marissa!" I said. "Do you remember me?"

"This is Dr. Hamilton," Abigail offered. "He helped you last week when your ear was hurting."

"How are you doing?" I asked.

"Good!" Marissa replied with a happy smile.

I complimented her on the pretty dress she was wearing, and the bright red sneakers on her feet.

"And how are *you*, Dr. Hamilton?" Abigail asked, while we stood beside each other pulling the hairy green husks back to examine the freshness of the cobs inside.

"Very well, thanks."

"Have you flushed any more spiders out of patients' ears since I last saw you?"

"Can't say that I have," I replied with a chuckle, "but I'm sure Marissa's spider won't be the last."

Abigail tossed another cob into the paper bag she had propped open on the pile, and leaned close to speak privately to me. "I just hope there won't be any latent symptoms of arachnophobia. I hope she doesn't start screaming every time she sees a bug."

"I don't think you have anything to worry about," I said. "She seems like a tough kid. She probably won't even remember what happened."

"But *I* will," Abigail replied with a shudder. "Pardon me for saying so, but it totally freaked me out. It's a good thing I didn't know what was in there, or you may have had to call in your nurse to hold me down, too."

I laughed. "You were good with her. She's a lucky girl."

Abigail was quiet for a moment while she peeled back another husk. "Thank you. I appreciate that. It hasn't been easy, the past year."

My speed at peeling husks slowed. Actually, I only wanted to purchase three because I was eating alone, but I now had six in my bag.

"Your husband…?" I gently asked.

She nodded. "He was a good man and a wonderful father. I never imagined I'd end up as a single mother."

"I'm sorry. Do you have family around here to help you?"

"Yes, thank goodness. My mother-in-law's a godsend. She moved in with us after Gordon died, so I was eventually able to return to work, and I didn't have to put Marissa in daycare. I don't know what I would have done without her."

"I'm glad to hear that," I replied. "What do you do?"

"I teach at the high school."

"What subject?"

"Art and English."

"Where did you go to school?" I asked, wondering if we might have been at Dal together.

"I got my degrees in Idaho," she explained. "That's where I'm from originally, but I have dual citizenship because of Gordon, who was from here. We met in Florida on spring break, believe it or not. I know...so cliché. We kept in touch and had a long-distance relationship, then got married and decided to settle here. I really love Canada, especially Nova Scotia. It's so laid back and everyone's so friendly. Drivers actually stop for you at crosswalks."

By now we had moved on from the corn bin, and were cruising the lettuce section.

"I know what you mean," I said. "I grew up in Toronto. Great city, but it's a very different world."

"And where did you go to school?"

I told her about Carleton and Dal, and she asked about my family. I explained that my father had died when I was very young, and that my mother still lived in Toronto, but we didn't keep in touch.

"She remarried a few years ago," I told her. "I attended her wedding, but that was the last time we saw each other. She's never been to Nova Scotia."

"And what about you?" Abigail said as she dropped two broccoli crowns into a plastic bag and tied it shut. "Are you married?"

"No. I work too much."

"Well that is something you should remedy," Abigail said. "Life is short, Dr. Hamilton. Enjoy every minute while you can."

This was not news to me, of course, for I was no stranger to death. Not only in my profession, but in my personal life as well.

"Words to live by," I said.

Abigail gestured over her shoulder. "You were buying a lot of corn back there. Big plans for dinner?"

"No, none," I replied. "I just like corn." I wasn't about to say that I had been distracted by every word she spoke, by the clean fruity fragrance of her shampoo, and those blue eyes that knocked me over every time she looked at me. On top of it all, I couldn't seem to tear myself away from Marissa, who was still sitting in the cart, politely listening to us as we conversed.

"I like corn, too!" she shouted gleefully, and we both laughed.

Abigail tickled her on the neck. "Yes, you do. And it's so good for you!" She turned to me. "Are you doing anything for supper, Dr. Hamilton? We'd love to have you join us if you're free. My mother-in-law will be there, and she's a terrific cook."

"First of all, I'm not your regular doctor, so you should call me Ryan. And thank you for the invitation. I accept."

Her eyebrows flew up. "Great. How about 6:00? Do you know where I live?"

I shook my head.

We stopped our carts and she dug into her purse for a pen and small notepad. She wrote down the address. "It's off the number 3, to your left if you're heading toward Mahone Bay." She ripped off the small sheet of paper and handed it to me.

I slipped it into my shirt pocket. "Thanks. I'll be there. Can I bring anything?"

"Just yourself," she said with a smile as she pushed her cart forward and headed toward the back of the store.

I couldn't help but watch her walk away from me. I liked how her hips swung under that silky pink and white sundress. I don't think any woman had ever sparked such a natural, immediate fascination in me. There was something so fresh and wholesome about her.

As they rounded the corner of the aisle, Marissa leaned out and waved at me. My heart leapt, and I waved back at her with a giddy smile.

It was Gladys Smith, Abigail's mother-in-law, who greeted me at the door. "Welcome, Dr. Hamilton! Come in, come in!" I crossed the threshold into a wide entrance hall with a view to a large bank of windows that looked out over the water. The floors were light birch hardwood, the walls were painted a clean taupe with white trim, and the furniture was casual, with soft, inviting white sofas and Mexican-styled throws.

"What a great spot," I said, handing Gladys two bottles of wine – a heavy cabernet and a light pinot grigio, just to cover all the bases.

"Thank you so much," she replied. "We love it here. It's quiet and private, and the yard is nice and big for Marissa to play in."

She escorted me along those immaculately polished floors to the back of the house, which was brightly lit by the sunshine streaming in through the windows. The living room was open to a large cream-colored kitchen to the right, where Abigail was stirring something on the stove. The smell of garlic and spices was intoxicating.

"Hello there." She turned slightly to look over her shoulder at me, and I was mesmerized again by those incredible blue eyes. "You found the place okay?"

"Yeah, no problem," I replied. "Great view." I looked out at the giant sky dotted with white clouds, and the choppy waters over the Bay below.

The house, covered in bleached gray cedar shakes and white trim, was perched high on a grassy hill with a deck that stretched all around.

Right away I noticed Marissa out on the deck playing in a green plastic sandbox shaped like a turtle. She wore a white sun-hat on her head.

"And look, he brought wine," Gladys said, setting both bottles on the shiny granite countertop on the center island. "What do you prefer, doctor? Red or white? Or how about a cocktail? Martini? Gin and tonic? Name your pleasure."

"I'll take a glass of water, please," I replied.

"Still or sparkling."

"Sparkling, if you have it."

"We have everything. Slice of lemon?"

"Sounds wonderful."

I sat down on one of the white leather bar stools at the kitchen island, while Gladys filled a tall crystal tumbler with ice and poured fizzing Perrier into it. Next came the lemon, and I was greatly refreshed.

"Abigail tells me you come from Toronto," Gladys said. "I hope we don't lose you to another big city. It's so hard to keep doctors here. Rural medicine isn't everyone's cup of tea, you know."

"I'm very happy here," I told her. "I enjoy the quiet here and the slower pace of life. I don't have any plans to leave, I assure you."

"Well, that's a relief. And it's nice to have a young doctor in town for a change. All we have are the old cronies who are only here to be close their luxury yachts."

"Gladys..." Abigail gave her a warning look. "I believe Dr. Hamilton also has a boat."

Gladys pierced me with her gaze. "Do you?"

"Yes," I replied, "but in my defense, it's a motor boat, and I bought it used."

Gladys threw up her hand. "Well, there! You see? You're not like those old cronies at all."

Abigail and I shared a knowing smirk.

"Not that there's anything wrong with boating," Gladys continued. "I love being out on the water. Don't you, Abigail?"

"Yes, I do," she replied as she slid sizzling butter-seared scallops onto a plate and set it on the island in front of me. "You're not allergic to seafood are you?"

"Heaven forbid," I replied, reaching for a toothpick. "Are you going to have some, too?" I asked Gladys.

"Good God, yes. Don't hog them all. Slide that plate this way."

Abigail poured herself a glass of white wine and stood at the island, where we all devoured the scallops while discussing the challenge of keeping emergency rooms open in rural hospitals. Then somehow we got talking about my life in Ontario and why I came east. Before a half hour had passed, I had told them both about my upbringing with a string of nannies and how I was a wild teenager before I straightened myself out.

Marissa stood up from the sandbox and came inside to join us.

Abigail went to meet her at the sliding glass door, scooped her into her arms, and kissed her on the cheek. "Would you like a drink of juice?" she asked. "And look who's here to see you. Dr. Hamilton."

Marissa's face lit up. She reached that sweet pudgy hand out to me and squirmed in her mother's arms. "Docca!"

Abigail set Marissa down so she could run to me. I rose from my chair, and before I knew it, I was lifting her up over my head, then squeezing her as if she were my own.

"My first name's Ryan," I said. "Can you say that?"

"Wyan," she replied with a grin.

I shared a look with Abigail, whose eyes were warm with pride and love, and I knew in that instant that she was nothing like the mother who had raised *me*.

Marissa was one lucky girl.

I married Abigail eleven months later. The ceremony was held in a small chapel in Chester. We invited her colleagues from work – the high school principal, administrative staff, and most of the teachers – and I invited my receptionist and the two other doctors in town, along with their wives.

My mother surprised me by coming all the way from Ontario, and she was charming and friendly toward Abigail and Gladys. I wasn't worried that she would make a poor impression. She was a successful businesswoman, after all, and she knew how to schmooze.

We held the reception at Abigail's home – which was now my home as well – in the backyard, overlooking the water. Abigail had never lived there with Gordon, so I wasn't encroaching on another man's territory. They had rented a place in town during their marriage, and she and Gladys bought the current house a year after he passed. I took over what was left of the mortgage, and Gladys continued to live with us in her own apartment downstairs.

I never felt as if Gladys resented me for stepping into her son's shoes, especially in the eyes of her only granddaughter, who had no memory of her real father. To the contrary, Gladys was grateful for my presence in Marissa's life, and she treated me like her own son.

She turned out to be the mother I'd never had.

How astounding that life can be so cruel one moment, and so generous the next.

Abigail and I were blissfully happy, and though we were unable to have children of our own — despite our greatest efforts and a parade of fertility treatments — we never once took for granted the blessing that was Marissa, for she was a shining, shimmering light in both our lives.

It was she who ultimately steered me in the direction I was meant to go.

I always knew she was a clever girl. I knew it the first moment I met her in my office when she was screaming about the pain in her ear. She had looked me in the eye with a wisdom I found astonishing for a child of that age. There was an awareness there…a confidence and a curiosity.

As a young child, she was physically active and adventurous, and though she exhausted us at times with her questions and energy, we were never anything but grateful and flabbergasted by her intelligence and zest for life. I knew enough about psychology to recognize that she was a gifted child, and the fact that we had no other children allowed us to give every ounce of ourselves to Marissa. Emotionally, intellectually, and financially. One of us – that included Gladys – was always available to read to her at night, to play thought-provoking games, and later, to help her with high-level math and science, history, French, and English.

I was the math and science expert, and Abigail was a master of the arts. Marissa was fully bilingual in English and French by the time she was ten, and could play the piano and violin.

For her part, Gladys provided a moral learning center. She volunteered at the food bank and nursing home, and when Marissa was old enough, Gladys taught her the value of charity and compassion.

When she reached high school, Marissa joined the student council and started a fund-raising campaign – a bottle run and walk-a-thon – to raise money for the children's hospital in Halifax. The first year, she helped raise a thousand dollars and appeared on live television to present the check. She did the same thing the next two years running, raising more money each year, before passing the baton to another high-achieving student after she graduated.

I was incredibly proud of her. But it doesn't end there. Her kindness, strength, and love provided a true inspiration to me at a time when the winds of destiny shifted yet again, and bad luck returned to my world.

Abigail and I had been married for fifteen wonderful years when Gladys put the DVD player in the dishwasher. There was nearly a house fire when, a few days later, she left a pot of carrots boiling on the stove, and decided to go for a walk. She lost her sense of direction on the beach, and by the time she found her way back home, the carrots had boiled dry, the kitchen was full of smoke, alarms were going off, and a neighbor had called the fire department.

I'm sure it will come as no surprise for you to learn that Gladys was eventually diagnosed with Alzheimer's. It wasn't easy dealing with the emotional impact. She was such an integral part of our lives. Now decisions had to be made about her future, and ours.

But it gets worse. One month after Gladys was diagnosed, Abigail found a lump in her breast.

I did everything I could as a husband, a son, and a doctor. Thank heavens Gladys was still in the early stages of her illness, and she was able to comprehend what was happening to Abigail. She was helpful and strong, and a great support for Abigail during treatments.

Marissa, who was seventeen at the time, was a rock for me that entire year, especially when Abigail had to have a double mastectomy. That was followed by aggressive chemotherapy, and it killed me to see my beautiful wife so ill. I wished that it could have been me instead of her.

It was traumatic for all of us, but we held strong together. We did everything to make sure Abigail was comfortable, full of hope, and felt loved every minute of each precious day.

We lost her after a nine-month battle against a very aggressive disease that had spread to nine of her lymph nodes.

It's not easy to talk about. Forgive me, but I simply cannot bear to describe the details of her death, or relive my emotions before, during, and after. I apologize. I am not a poet. All I can say is that I lost my best friend, my lover, my soul mate, and my hero that year, for she had rescued me from a life of solitude, and showed me what it meant to be part of a loving family. For that – and for *her* – I will always be grateful.

A New Perspective

Forty-two

Marissa

"I think we should get some help," I said to Ryan, my step-dad, when I came home to Chester for the summer after my third year at university.

I was attending Dalhousie in Halifax, which was Ryan's alma mater – but I always returned to Chester for the summers to spend time with him and Gram, and to work at the yacht club, where I was an instructor in the sailing school for kids.

I was now twenty years old, and my mother Abigail had been gone for two.

"What kind of help?" Ryan asked.

I pulled a couple of mugs down from the cupboard, set them on the counter, and went searching for teabags. "A geriatric home care worker," I said, "and I think we should try and find someone while I'm here this summer, so I can make sure we don't get stuck with some lazy psycho. I want the very best for Gram."

The way I saw it – someone had to be here to keep an eye on her while we were both at work, and that person would require nursing skills, because Gram was starting to lose her ability to do certain things on her own.

She was also waking up disoriented during the night and wandering around the house as if she were lost. Ryan and I were both exhausted.

Looking weary after a long day at the clinic, Ryan sat down at the kitchen island and cupped his forehead in a hand. "Your mother always imagined she would be the one to take care of Gladys, right up until the end. It would break her heart to know that we were hiring a stranger to look after her."

I dropped the teabags into the cups and drowned them in steaming water from the kettle. "Not a stranger," I said. "A responsible home care worker who will be a friend to us, as long as we find the right person." I placed his mug in front of him.

I watched him take hold of the paper tab and dip the teabag for a few seconds. His eyes lifted, and he looked at me. "I'm glad you're home. It's been rough here without you. I don't know how I'll manage in September when you go back."

"That's why we need to get someone *now*," I told him. "I can help with the search."

I saw his Adam's apple bob, then my eyes darted to the doorway that led downstairs to Gram's basement apartment.

She was standing there in her nightgown and slippers, staring at us.

"Don't you think I should be part of this discussion?" she asked.

My stomach dropped. I was both mortified and concerned for her feelings. "Of course, Gram. Come on over."

She shuffled across the floor and sat on the stool next to Ryan. "Yes, thank you. I would love a cup a tea. How kind of you to offer."

We both chuckled, and Ryan slid his mug across to her. I went to pour him a replacement.

"You were always such a gentleman," she said with a wink. "That's why Abby married you, and she made a darn good choice. Wish I could say the same for myself." She was referring to her own marriage, which had ended in divorce around the time Abigail married my real dad. "What were we talking about?" Gladys asked.

I knew she'd heard what I said about hiring a home care worker, but it wasn't uncommon for her to forget the thread of a conversation. "We were just discussing the bingo hall," I said. "They need air conditioning, don't you think?"

Gladys regarded me over the rim of her teacup as she took a sip. "Don't play games with me, young lady. I may not remember who the Prime Minister is, but I know when I'm being talked about. You're trying to figure out what to do with me."

Ryan laid a hand on her shoulder. "We're not going to 'do' anything with you, Gladys. We love you, and we're going to take care of you. Right here."

She set down her mug. "I love you, too, but I won't have either of you feeling sorry for me. I've had a great life, and I intend to enjoy what time I have left – while I can still remember who the heck you are. But in order for me to enjoy it, I need to know that you are both going to take care of *yourselves*."

She directed her gaze back at Ryan. "I know you haven't been sleeping because you've been up with me, making sure I don't step off a cliff and fall into the Bay, but if you're going to take care of me, you need to stay healthy. So yes, hire someone. I'd like to be involved, if you don't mind, since he or she will be helping me in and out of the bathtub before long."

"Gram––" I said, surprised by how lucid and sensible she was in that moment. I wanted to apologize for making her feel as if we didn't think her opinion mattered.

She held up a hand. "No, you have to listen to me, because I probably won't remember to tell you this later. When the time comes to put me in a home, I want you to do it, and not feel guilty about it. Do you understand? I know what lies ahead for me, and I don't want to be a burden to either one of you. Yes, hire someone to babysit me now, especially at night, but when it becomes more than that…"

Ryan put his arm around her, pulled her close, and kissed the top of her head.

My throat closed up. Swallowing hard, I moved around the island to join them. "I can't imagine you not living here with us," I said to Gram.

"But there will come a time when it's necessary," she replied. "When the time is right, you'll know. And it will be okay. I promise."

We continued to hug around the kitchen island, until she told us to stop blubbering and turn on the television. Oh, how she loved the Discovery Channel.

But Gram was a creature of habit, so she woke us again at 3:00 a.m., and it wasn't easy getting her back to bed. She thought she was in a strange house and wanted desperately to go home where she would be safe.

We began the search for the perfect home care worker the following day.

We were fortunate in that Ryan knew all the right questions to ask the agencies, and he was able to get some excellent recommendations. We would have loved to find someone local, but the person Gram liked the best lived in Halifax, so we chose to pay her extra in order for her to relocate to Chester.

Again, we were fortunate because Ryan earned a good income, the house was paid off, and we still had a nest egg left over from my father's life insurance policy.

We offered the candidate of our choice a rent-free flat to live in. It didn't have a view of the water, but we provided a membership to the yacht club, access to Ryan's boat, and in addition, we promised a generous biweekly stipend if the candidate agreed to be on call during the weekends.

To our delight, Elizabeth Jackson accepted the position, but we had to wait two weeks for her to start, because she was employed at a nursing home in the city and insisted on giving proper notice.

In the meantime, we were able to hire a local home care worker to cover the night shift from 11:00 to 7:00 in the morning. His name was Justin. He was a handsome young nursing assistant with a terrific sense of humor, which Gram appreciated when she found herself trying to figure out the lock on the back door at 3:00 a.m.

Ryan took the next two weeks off work to stay home with Gram during the days, while we waited for Elizabeth to arrive.

When she walked through the door, however, Ryan took one look at her from the top of the stairs and frowned at me.

While Gram took Elizabeth out onto the deck to show her the view, he quickly descended the stairs, dragged me by the arm into the kitchen pantry, and slid the door shut.

"Are you kidding me?" he said in an angry whisper. "We offer a salary and benefits worthy of an ER doc, and you hire *that*? She looks like she's having an identity crisis. She doesn't know if she wants to be a goth or a motorcycle chick."

"She's the one Gram wanted!" I replied in my defence, because I, too, had had my doubts when Elizabeth Jackson first walked into the coffee shop in Halifax where Gram and I held the interview. She won me over, however, as soon as she smiled and spoke.

Ryan had been working that day, so he'd left it up to us to conduct the interviews. He told me it would be a good experience for me.

"You're telling me that woman is a certified nurse's aid?" Ryan said. "She has a *tattoo*."

"It's a butterfly," I argued, as if that made a difference. "And it's on her wrist."

He let out a breath. "It's still a tattoo. She's got to be pushing forty, for pity's sake. If she was seventeen, I might be able to excuse it, but..." He paused. "How long has she had it?"

"The tattoo? I don't know. It didn't seem like an appropriate question to ask. And she's not forty. She's thirty-seven. It was on her resume. Didn't you read it?"

He raked his fingers through his hair, then rested his hands on his hips. "Geez. What are we going to do? I don't think she's going to work out."

"Why not?" I practically shouted. "You haven't even talked to her yet. She's a very nice person."

His chest heaved. "She's not what I expected. How do we know she's not going to rob us blind?"

"Why? Because she has a tattoo?"

"And spiky black hair," he added, as if that was the icing on the cake.

"She's wearing a dress," I offered.

"With combat boots."

I stared at him for a moment, then couldn't help but burst out laughing. "What is wrong with you? You're not usually so judgemental."

"I don't know," he replied. "Something about her just rubs me the wrong way. She doesn't look like a home care worker."

"What did you expect? Someone in white pants and a white shirt? With those ugly white leather loafers? God, you have me picturing Nurse Ratched in *One Flew Over the Cuckoo's Nest*. I promise you, Elizabeth is nothing like that. She had excellent references from the nursing home where she worked. And she's creative. That's what Gram loves about her."

"*How* is she creative?" Ryan asked.

"She paints watercolors."

"Of what? Dead seagulls?"

I laughed again. "You are too much, Ryan. Just relax. Everything's going to be fine. You'll like her once you get to know her. Now let's get out of here before she figures out we're hiding in the pantry closet. Then *we'll* be the ones committed to a home."

I pushed the sliding pantry door open. We crossed the kitchen and stepped out onto the sunny, breezy deck where Gram was chatting with the already tarnished home care worker with the butterfly tattoo.

—⌒○

"Elizabeth," I said, "this is my stepdad, Ryan Hamilton."

Elizabeth held out her hand. "Nice to meet you, Dr. Hamilton. You have a beautiful home."

There, see? The spiky-haired home worker exhibits excellent social graces.

Ryan shook her hand and greeted her with a warm smile, behaving as if the conversation we'd just had in the pantry closet had never occurred. How thankful I was, in that moment, that he, too, could exhibit excellent social graces.

"Nice to meet you, as well," he said. "You've been working in a seniors' home, I'm told."

"Yes, I was mostly involved in organizing social activities and crafts. Every Wednesday night we had a jazz band come in, and I loved getting the residents up to dance."

"Are you a dancer?" Gram asked.

Elizabeth chuckled. "Not really. I took jive lessons once, years ago, which came in handy on jazz night. You'd be surprised at how some of the residents can move. I could barely keep up sometimes."

"That sounds like so much fun." I turned to Ryan. "Didn't I always say you and Mom should take ballroom dancing classes together?"

"I wish we'd had the chance."

An awkward silence ensued, until Gram started backing up. Soon she was doing the two-step around the deck. "Lessons!" she shouted. "Who needs lessons? Some of us are naturals. Watch and learn, young ones."

Elizabeth laughed, hooted, and applauded.

"Gram!" I called out to her, raising my thumb and pinky to my ear and mouth. "The phone is ringing. It's Tom Bergeron from *Dancing With the Stars!*"

Ryan watched Gram for a few seconds, then crossed toward her, held out his hand, and started singing "Only You." She stepped into his arms and they waltzed together around the perimeter of the wide deck.

"You're beautiful," Elizabeth said to them.

I glanced at her in the sunshine while the breeze blew a part in her short black hair, and felt an immediate connection to her, which I couldn't begin to explain.

In that moment, it was obvious – at least to me – that we had chosen the right candidate, and I knew it wouldn't take long for Ryan to realize it, too.

CHAPTER

Forty-four

❦

The following day, while I was working at the yacht club, Elizabeth took Gram down to the beach where they hunted for seashells and unique rocks. When I returned at suppertime and walked through the front door, I breathed in the delectable aroma of creamy seafood chowder, warm bread in the oven, and boiled corn on the cob. I had to stop for a moment, close my eyes, and inhale as deeply as I could, for it was a heady fragrance. "Wow. That smells fantastic."

Elizabeth, who was stirring the pot of chowder at the stove, turned and smiled at me. "I was told you aren't allergic to seafood."

"Heavens no. I'm a Maritimer. I have lobster in my blood." I glanced to my left and saw Gram sitting on the sofa in the living room, leaning forward over something on the coffee table. "Whatcha doin', Gram?"

I dropped my keys on the kitchen island and went to kiss her on the cheek. She leaned back to look up at me.

"Behold," she said, sweeping a hand over three smooth beach rocks the size of ostrich eggs that lay on the table. She must have spent the entire afternoon painting them. I admired the colors and images she had created. One stone was blue with swirly textures, like ocean waves. Another was clearly intended to be a butterfly.

"You've been busy," I replied with fascination. I sat down on the sofa cushion and put my arm around her shoulders. "They're wonderful." I examined each one. "What should we do with them?"

"We should put them in the rose garden at the edge of the yard," she suggested. "I think that's a good place, don't you?"

"Overlooking the Bay," I replied. "It's perfect."

Gram beamed.

"They're beautiful," I said. "And this one has glitter."

I felt Elizabeth approach us from behind. Though she wore no shoes and made no sound, I knew she was standing over us even before she spoke.

I turned and smiled up at her. "You must have brought the paints?"

"Yes," she replied. "When it comes to art supplies, I am very well stocked."

I nodded. "This is wonderful, thank you. Can I paint one?" I asked Gram.

"Sure!" She pointed at the steel bucket in front of the fireplace. "We collected a boatload."

I laughed. "That bucket must have weighed a ton, hauling it up here!"

"We each carried some," Elizabeth explained, "and made a few trips throughout the day, so it wasn't that bad."

"I wish I could have joined you," I said.

"You always loved walking on the beach," Gram mentioned. "Remember when you were little?"

"You took me every day," I replied, feeling a tremendous wave of love wash over me, for Gladys and my parents, Ryan and Abigail, had given me the best childhood a girl could ask for.

Raising Gram's frail, blue-veined hand to my lips, I kissed it and held it against my cheek.

If only she could be a part of my life forever.

Why do people have to go?

The love in her eyes told me she remembered all the joy and laughter from our lives, and she, too, felt blessed and fulfilled.

"I'm so glad we can be together," she said. "We are lucky, aren't we?"

I was very aware that Elizabeth had watched our exchange with tender but aching envy, before she quietly backed away and returned to the pot of chowder on the stove.

"The beach rocks are great," Ryan said to me that evening after Elizabeth went home.

We had all eaten dinner together, but as soon as I stood to clear the table, Gram said she felt tired and wanted to go to bed. Ryan and I insisted that Elizabeth should not have to stay to help with the cleanup. She had already worked more than her scheduled hours for the day.

"I love the rocks, too," I replied as I bent to load the chowder bowls into the dishwasher. "Didn't I tell you Elizabeth was a good choice? Gram said she was a lovely companion today, and I really think the painting is a wonderful creative outlet. It'll be good for her to have a way to express herself when she starts to lose her language ability. She'll find joy in that. I know she will."

Ryan put the butter and salad dressings in the fridge. "I agree. And it was nice of Elizabeth to cook us this meal. She didn't have to. It's not part of her job description. *Or is it?*"

"No. But she said she wants to fit in like a family friend, so that Gram feels comfortable with her – especially later on, when she might forget who she's actually related to."

We were both quiet for a moment. "That makes sense," he said.

I closed the dishwasher door and pressed the start button. The motor quietly began to hum.

"How was she today?" Ryan asked.

I faced him. "Who? Gram or Elizabeth?"

"Gram," he replied with a smirk. "Were there any major incidents? No car keys or lamps discovered in the freezer?"

I chuckled. "No. It was a good day. Uneventful. Elizabeth said she'd call if there were any problems, but you can just read the report if you want to know everything that went on."

"There's a report?" he said, lifting an eyebrow.

"Yes, right over there." I pointed.

Ryan went to the counter area under the microwave, and flipped open the binder. "Doesn't she know how to use a laptop?"

"She prefers loose leaf and longhand. She's not the techie type, or haven't you noticed?"

"She has a cell phone," he mentioned.

"But it's a dinosaur – one of those flip-phones with just a number keypad. She only uses it for talking. With her *voice*. No texting. No Twitter."

"Wow." He leaned back against the counter and folded his arms across his chest. "I gotta say, I admire her fortitude."

"She told me she likes to live life in the moment with her head up, not with her eyes down, fixed on a screen."

Ryan nodded again. "I like that idea."

"Yeah, me, too. We could all use a little less screen time. Want to go into town and get some ice cream?"

"I'd love to," he replied, pushing away from the counter, "but we shouldn't leave Gram alone. How about you go buy a tub and bring it home."

He picked up his car keys, twirled them around his forefinger, and tossed them to me.

"Do you think Elizabeth will cook for us every night?" he asked.

"I don't know," I replied as I opened the door. "Maybe you should ask her."

A week later, I invited Elizabeth to stay late and watch an old Demi Moore movie on television – *About Last Night*. Elizabeth was officially off duty in the evenings, so we decided to have a girls' night in and make popcorn.

Elizabeth brought the popcorn. It was the organic kind, and she popped it on the stove with an equal mixture of olive and canola oils. It was the best popcorn I'd ever tasted.

Ryan was on call at the hospital, and Gram had gone to bed early, as she did most nights. I told Justin, the night shift worker, not to come until midnight because we had Gram covered. He was happy to have some extra time off – with pay, of course.

When the credits started to roll, I had to pass Elizabeth a tissue.

"I forgot how much I love that movie," she said. "I was in high school when I first saw it."

"It's a great film," I agreed. "And who doesn't love Jim Belushi? He was brilliant in this."

She inhaled deeply. "I suppose I should get going, but let me help you clean up first."

She picked up the empty popcorn bowl, and I collected our water glasses. Together we moved into the kitchen and piled everything on the counter at the sink.

"Have you decided what you're going to do after you graduate?" Elizabeth asked as she squirted dish soap into the popcorn bowl and filled it with sudsy water.

"I have a few different interests," I replied, "but this is my last year at Dal, so I'll have to choose something."

"What are your options?" She reached for the water glasses and gently dipped them into the water.

I pulled a clean dishtowel out of the drawer. "I want to do something in the health professions, so I'm thinking about occupational therapy, physiotherapy, or maybe even medical school."

"Like your dad. How are your marks?"

"Straight A's," I replied, "but after what's been happening with Gram, I'm also considering a nursing degree. Maybe I could specialize in geriatrics and work in a nursing home."

Elizabeth nodded. "That all sounds great. I don't think there's any wrong decision."

"That's why it's so hard to choose. Part of me would like to work with elderly patients and just take care of them on a daily basis, you know? But another part of me is fascinated with the science of what's happening to Gram. I've been reading a lot about Alzheimer's lately, and I might like to do something on the research side."

Elizabeth rinsed a glass under the running water and handed it to me. I dried it with the towel and set it upside down in the cupboard.

"What about boys?" Elizabeth asked. "Any handsome young men in your life?"

I sighed. "Not at the moment. I've had a few relationships, but nothing has ever stuck. The first one lasted just over a year," I told her. "That was in high school. His name was Robert and he works at one of the golf courses in Halifax now. We're still friends."

"That's nice." She rinsed and handed me the second glass.

"Then I dated a guy my first year at Dal. That also lasted about a year, but he cheated on me, so that was the end of that."

"I'm sorry to hear that."

"Yeah, well, what are you going to do?"

"Dump him," she said, giving me a playful nudge.

I chuckled. "Damn straight."

While Elizabeth washed the popcorn bowl, I stood quietly, admiring her profile under the bright halogen sink lights. She was an attractive woman with a tiny upturned nose and expressive eyes. She kind of reminded me of Nicole Kidman, except for the cropped black hair. And she was not as tall. Elizabeth was very petite.

She had such an inherent kindness about her, and a sense of calm and optimism that I respected and appreciated. "You remind me of my mom sometimes," I said, out of the blue.

Her lips curled into a barely discernible smile, as if she were touched by the comment. Then she looked at me with those caring eyes. "You must miss her a lot."

"I do. She was an amazing woman and a superstar as a mother. I always felt loved, as if I were the most important thing in the world to her."

"I'm sure you were." She handed me the popcorn bowl, and I dried it while she washed the cutlery we had used. "What about your real father?" she asked. "How old were you when——"

"I never really knew him," I explained. "He died when I was less than a year old. What about you? Are you close to your parents?"

She pulled the stopper in the sink to let the water drain. "I was closer to my mom than my dad. He was too…" She paused. "Strict. We certainly had our differences. He just didn't agree with some of the choices I made in my youth. I ended up rebelling. Then, in my twenties, I didn't speak to either of my parents for almost five years. Then Mom got sick. Kind of like your mom."

"Was it breast cancer?" I asked with concern.

"Ovarian. She passed away ten years ago."

"I'm sorry."

Elizabeth nodded appreciatively.

I was hesitant to ask any more questions, because I sensed from the start that Elizabeth didn't enjoy sharing information about her personal life, especially her youth. Something told me she wasn't proud of her past. I was curious about her, however. I wanted to know everything – every last intimate detail.

"What about your dad?" I dared to ask while she wiped the top of the island with the dishcloth. "Are you close to him now?"

She shrugged. "I wouldn't say 'close.' We do keep in touch. Occasionally. Maybe once a year."

I leaned against the counter. "Do you have any brothers or sisters?"

"No, it's just me." She folded the dishcloth and placed it on the back corner of the sink.

A quiet knock rapped at the door. I glanced at the clock on the microwave.

"It's midnight," I said. "That must be Justin."

Elizabeth grabbed her sweater and picked up her purse while I went to answer the door.

"Hi, Justin. Come on in," I said.

Unlike Elizabeth, he wore a white uniform that made him look every inch the hospital worker.

"How was the movie?" he asked as he stepped inside.

I closed the door behind him. "It was great."

"Hi, Justin," Elizabeth said. "I'm just on my way out. Have a good night."

She waved at me and was gone before I had a chance to say anything other than, "See you tomorrow."

Later, when I slipped between the cool sheets in my bed, I couldn't stop thinking about our conversation in the kitchen, and what she'd said about the choices she had made in her youth, which caused her to become estranged from her parents for five years.

What were those choices? I wondered. And what sort of life had she lived before coming to work with us?

Then I thought about Ryan and the choices *he* had made in his youth. He had never hidden any of that from me. As soon as I was old enough to understand – and a few of my classmates began experimenting with drugs and alcohol – he told me about his childhood and his difficult adolescence, and spared none of the more tragic details, including what happened to his friends.

I must have been twelve or thirteen at the time, and I always admired how he'd managed to turn his life around, when it could have been so different from what it is now.

I was thankful he ended up with us. Thankful for that spider in my ear. Thankful for the corn bin at the grocery store.

Tonight, I told Elizabeth that she reminded me of my mother, and it was true, in many ways. But the more I thought about the difficult adolescence she had described, the more I realized she had much more in common with Ryan.

The month of July passed in a full bloom of pink and red roses, yellow-petaled brown-eyed Susans, and a collage of other flowers that painted our yard in vivid splashes of color. Elizabeth said that when she and Gram sat on the back deck, sipping iced tea on sunny afternoons, she imagined the gardens were the foreground in a Monet painting, and the sailboats in the distance on the choppy blue bay were joyful brush strokes of whimsy.

I asked if she was interested in using Ryan's boat, but she said boating was not something she would attempt alone. I suggested she invite some friends down to visit some weekend, but since she had agreed to be on call for us, she said she preferred to be on land and available, just in case.

As for Gram, she painted hundreds of beach stones that summer. As August drew to a close, just before I returned to school, we decided to hold a yard sale on a Saturday, sell most of them for five dollars each, and donate the entire proceeds to our favorite charity – the IWK Children's Hospital in Halifax.

I spread the word in town and stapled posters to telephone poles. I also sent an email to *The Chronicle Herald*, and a reporter showed up the morning of the sale to do a story on Gram. Ryan barbequed hot dogs that we sold for a buck each. We raised just over two thousand dollars.

When Labor Day weekend rolled around, I was eager to get back to my studies and my friends at school, but uneasy about leaving Ryan, Gram, and Elizabeth, because if the summer had taught me anything – it was that life was precious, and family, even more so. It was not going to be easy to say good-bye, and I dreaded what changes might take place while I was gone.

───⸜

On my last night at home, we decided to barbeque my favorite: filet steaks rubbed with sea salt, potato salad with mustard and diced celery, roasted red peppers, and steamed asparagus with butter.

Gram handled the potato salad – it was her specialty – while I took care of the other vegetables. Ryan, as always, was master of the barbeque.

We invited Elizabeth to join us, and she arrived wearing a white sundress I'd never seen on her before, and a pair of turquoise Roman sandals – a noticeable change from the worn-out combat boots she always wore. Her toenails were painted pale pink.

Aside from the outfit, there was something else different about her, but at first I wasn't quite sure what it was.

"I brought you a key lime pie," she said, raising it up when I greeted her at the door.

I felt my face light up. "How wonderful! Thank you. Allow me to take it out of your hands. I *love* key lime pie. Come on in. We're just finishing up the potato salad, and Ryan's out on the deck scraping the grill and listening to reggae music. I think he needs someone to talk to. Would you like a glass of wine or beer?"

"Iced tea would be great, if you have it," she replied.

"I'll bring it out to you."

She kissed Gram on the cheek, snuck a stick of celery from the cutting board, and pushed the sliding glass door open. Stepping out onto the deck, she said hello to Ryan, and slid the door closed behind her.

After I delivered Elizabeth's iced tea to her and gave Ryan a refill as well, Gram and I continued to work on the salad and veggies. Every once in a while, I glanced out the windows. Ryan and Elizabeth were chatting comfortably with each other, and I wished I could be a fly on the cedar shakes out there, and listen to their conversation.

"They're such a nice couple," Gram said.

I turned my gaze to her. "Yes, they are, aren't they?" It was the first time either of us had ever suggested anything like that so openly, though I can't deny I'd thought about it more than once over the summer.

"How long have they been married?" Gram asked.

I stopped what I was doing and set down my paring knife. Without answering the question, I watched her for a moment. She was staring dreamily out the windows.

"Gram?" I said. "How are you feeling?"

Her eyes turned to me, but there was something vacant in them. "I'm fine, dear," she replied.

She had never called me 'dear' in my entire life. At least not that I could remember.

I picked up my paring knife and continued hollowing out the red peppers but I kept an eye on her.

"Do they have children?" she asked, and I looked up again.

"Who?"

"The couple on the deck."

My heart started to race, and I swallowed uneasily. "No, Gram, they don't."

"What a shame," she said. "They're both so nice looking."

"Yes...they are," I replied, choosing not to correct her while I finished preparing the red peppers to slide into the oven.

It was an exceptionally warm evening for September. There was not a single breath of wind, so we ate at the table on the deck. Gram returned to her normal self and no longer seemed confused about Ryan and Elizabeth. She talked about how much she was going to miss me when I returned to school, and the only evidence of her memory loss occurred when she started to sing "Yellow Submarine," and stopped after the first few bars.

"I can't remember the next line," she said, then she leaned back in her chair and swirled her index finger next to her ear. "Big surprise! It's a miracle I didn't put rocks in the salad!"

We all laughed with her, and I was thankful she could keep a sense of humor through all this. That would take her – and all of us – a long way in the coming months.

Suddenly, as I thought about the future, it felt as if the clouds were whizzing by, the hands on the clocks were spinning around like whirligigs, and the crickets were chirping at double time.

I wanted to shout at the planet, order it to stop turning. I wanted the rivers to cease flowing...for everything to grind to a halt and remain just as it was.

None of that was possible, I knew, because tomorrow I would leave, and Gram would be different when I returned.

CHAPTER

Forty-seven

After dinner, Elizabeth's car wouldn't start. Ryan tried to give her a boost but he couldn't get the engine to turn over.

"It's probably the alternator," he said, lifting his head from under the hood and coiling the booster cables around his arm. He placed them in the back of his Jeep, then lowered both hoods. "I'll call Jimmy in the morning. I'm sure he won't mind coming by."

"Who's Jimmy?" Elizabeth asked.

"The best mechanic in town," Ryan replied, rubbing his palms over his thighs.

"That would be great. Thank you. But I still need to get home tonight."

Ryan and I both spoke up at the same time. "I'll drive you."

Elizabeth glanced from me to him, then back at me again.

"Why don't *you* take her," Ryan said.

"Unless *you* want to," I replied.

"No, no. You should enjoy one last chance to get behind the wheel, because it'll be Metro Transit for you for the next eight months."

I sighed and rolled my eyes, then turned to Elizabeth. "I'll just grab my purse."

Inside, Gram was watching television.

"I'm going to run Elizabeth home," I said. "Her car won't start."

"All right, dear," she replied, and because of her vacant look I wondered if she understood who Elizabeth was. Or who *I* was, for that matter.

"Ryan will be right in."

She gave no reply, so I went out the front door. Ryan was leaning back against his Jeep with one ankle crossed over the other, and Elizabeth was rubbing a hand over the back of her bare neck and nodding at whatever he was saying.

"Ready?" I asked as I reached them.

Elizabeth touched Ryan briefly on the arm. "I'll see you tomorrow."

"Yeah, have a good night," he casually replied, stepping away from the side of his Jeep and taking the front steps two at a time to the door.

Was that an extra special, jovial spring in his step? I wondered with a small grin as I got into the driver's seat and inserted the keys in the ignition.

Elizabeth got in beside me and set her purse on the floor. "Ryan said you were in need of a fridge for your dorm room. I have one I'm not using if you want it. We can pick it up now."

"That would be great. Thanks." I backed out of the driveway and headed into town. "Actually, I'm glad to have this time with you. I wanted to tell you about something that happened with Gram tonight, while you and Ryan were on the deck."

I explained how Gram mentioned what a nice couple they made and asked how long they were married, and if they had children.

"Oh dear," Elizabeth said.

"Yeah, it kind of caught me off guard. It's the first time she's ever done that – not recognized one of us."

Elizabeth was quiet for a moment. "I think this is the biggest challenge most people face when a family member gets Alzheimer's. It's hard not to take it personally when they don't remember you or even recognize you. But you have to remember that she does love you and she always has."

"I know," I said. "I won't ever begrudge her for this, and neither will Ryan. We understand what's happening to her. I'm more worried for *her* happiness. Won't she feel confused and alone if no one is familiar to her?"

"I won't lie to you, Marissa. There will be times when she'll be frightened. We'll just do our best to treat her with kindness and compassion. She'll feel it from us. Everything will be lived in the moment. There will be no past to count as a reference for her. Though she will likely continue to remember things from a very long time ago."

I took a deep breath and gripped the steering wheel tightly in my hands. "I don't feel right leaving Ryan alone to deal with this."

"He won't be alone. I'll be here too."

I turned my eyes to her. "Thank you. I don't know what we'd do without you."

A short while later I pulled into the driveway of her apartment, which was on the second floor of a converted house. "I'm going to miss you," I said.

"I'll miss you, too." We got out of the car. "But Thanksgiving will be here before you know it," she said. "Now come on up, and I'll dig that fridge out of my closet."

I followed her up the stairs and through the front door. "This is nice," I said, looking around at the cozy living room with Dijon-colored walls and soft upholstered chairs covered in pillows and fleece throw blankets.

A cat appeared out of nowhere and rubbed up against my legs. "Hello there." I bent down to scoop her into my arms. "What's your name?"

"That's Marie Curie." Elizabeth pulled her purse off over her head and set it on a chair at the table. "But I just call her Marie."

"Reincarnated, no doubt." I scratched behind Marie's ears. She purred and threw her head back in ecstasy. "She's adorable."

"And she knows it," Elizabeth informed me with a grin.

I set Ms. Curie down on the braided rug and followed Elizabeth into her bedroom to look for the fridge. She opened the closet door.

"There; what do you think? Is it too small?"

"No, it's perfect. You're sure you don't mind me borrowing it?"

"Not at all. It's just taking up space here. Let me help you carry it down to the Jeep."

I bent to pick it up, but abruptly straightened. "Actually, can I use your washroom first? I don't think I'll be able to make it home without a pit stop." I had sipped too much iced tea at supper.

"Of course," Elizabeth said. "It's right through there."

I found my way into her bathroom and used the facilities, then washed my hands, looked in the mirror, and noticed my mascara had smudged under my eyes.

I tugged a tissue out of the dispenser, wrapped it around my finger, and wet it under the faucet. I wiped away the dark shadow and leaned over the side of the sink to toss the crumpled tissue into the wastebasket.

Something caught my eye, and I frowned.

It was wrong of me, I openly admit that, but I simply couldn't help myself. I squatted down low and picked up the wastebasket to get a better look.

By the time I arrived home, Gram was in bed and Ryan was sitting up at the computer reading some news items from the day.

"Did you get the fridge?" he asked absently, without looking up.

I laid my hand on his shoulder. "Yes, but I came home with something else. Something just as interesting. More so in fact. It's in my purse. Want to see?"

He swiveled in his chair to face me. "First of all, let me be clear that I have never considered a mini fridge to be 'interesting,' but you have my attention."

I squinted mischievously at him and pulled five little squares of cream-colored paper out of the side compartment of my purse.

His eyebrows pulled together in a studious frown as he leaned forward in the chair. "I don't get it. What are these?"

"Temporary tattoos," I told him. "I found them in Elizabeth's trash can, along with a whole box of unused ones in the medicine cabinet."

He took hold of the one I held out. "It's the butterfly."

"Yes. She must put these on like blush or eyeliner every morning before she leaves her apartment. Who *does* that?"

He stood up and took one of the butterfly papers to examine it more closely. "So she doesn't actually have a tattoo?"

I shook my head. "She probably bought these at Claire's, in the teenybopper section."

"But why?" he asked. "I mean...why not get a real one if you're going to wash it off and stick a new one on every day?"

"Good question," I said. "Maybe you should ask her."

He handed it back to me. "No. This is her business and her private property. You shouldn't have taken it. Let's not mention it again."

"But aren't you curious?" I asked.

He turned away from me and pressed the button on the computer screen to shut it off for the night.

"Aren't you wondering why she would bother with something like this?" I continued when he didn't answer my first question.

He faced me and shook his head. "It's none of our business, Marissa."

"It is when we're trusting her with Gram's welfare."

He considered that for a moment. "Elizabeth is a good worker," he firmly said, "and Gladys loves her. That's all that matters."

With more than a little frustration – for now there was so much more I wanted to know about Elizabeth Jackson – I watched Ryan walk out on me and go upstairs to bed.

Curiosity

Forty-nine

c⌒c⌒ɔ⌒ɔ

Ryan

I t wasn't easy to say good-bye to Marissa that September. I never found it easy, especially after losing Abigail, but this time, watching her hug Gladys in the driveway was more than I could bear.

As I shifted the Jeep into reverse, and backed out, Marissa waved out the car window at Gladys and Elizabeth, then cried a steady flow of tears until we reached the highway junction.

She tried to convince me that she should take the year off, but I wouldn't hear of it. I assured her that Gladys would be appalled at the notion. Marissa's success at school was a great source of pleasure and pride for Gladys, and it was important that we honor that.

And so, the first few days without my stepdaughter at home passed with a discernible, gloomy silence in the house – for Marissa always brought such joy and laughter wherever she went.

On the fourth day, Elizabeth mentioned how quiet it was without Marissa. She looked at me curiously as we cleared the dishes from the table and asked how I was doing. I told her I was fine.

Then she offered to stay a bit and help load the dishwasher.

I didn't want to take advantage of her generosity, so I insisted that she go home and relax.

She asked if I was sure.

I said yes, so she left.

Thirty seconds later, she came back inside, pulled her purse off over her head, tossed it onto the computer chair, and said, "If you don't mind, I'd prefer to help with the dishes."

I stared at her for a long moment. "That would be great."

Without a word, she began to fill the sink while I loaded the dishwasher.

Elizabeth and I fell into a comfortable routine after that first week. Though she had been cooking for us and eating with us all summer, she always went home as soon as the table was cleared. Now she stayed until about 9:00 each night. She played cards or watched television with Gladys and me, then helped Gladys downstairs to bed.

Gladys adored her.

"Sometimes I wonder if Abigail sent you to me," Gladys said to Elizabeth one evening. "Like a guardian angel."

"Maybe she did," Elizabeth replied with fondness.

I appreciated Elizabeth just as ardently, though I kept my feelings to myself, for she was under my employ and I didn't want to jeopardize the precious household dynamic we had all come to enjoy.

Sometimes I pondered the situation on and off, for hours on end. I wasn't sure what I had ever done to deserve the blessing that had come to us in the form of Elizabeth Jackson. God knows I'd made my share of mistakes. So I figured I was just a fortunate beneficiary of a reward that was directed at Gladys.

Fifty

❦

I did not forget about the temporary tattoos Marissa had found in Elizabeth's apartment the night before she left for school. When she showed them to me I had responded with indifference, and was careful to remind her that the contents of Elizabeth's trash can was none of our business.

In all honesty, however, I was equally curious. I often found myself staring at that butterfly on the inside of Elizabeth's slender wrist, wondering how she managed to apply it in the exact same position each day, for I knew the precise location of every charming blue vein within the angle of the butterfly's wing span.

Many times I came close to asking her about it, but I always refrained, because I didn't want to catch her in a lie if she tried to hide the fact that it wasn't real.

On the other hand, if she told me the truth…Well, that would change things. It would mean she was sharing something private and personal with me, and I just didn't want to go there. I wasn't ready for that.

Looking back on it now, however, I suspect there was a part of me that suspected that, in time, I would be. It felt inevitable, like a giant ocean wave, a half mile out, visible from the beach, slowly making its way to shore.

cᴄᴄ⌇ᴐᴐ

Marissa planned to come home for Thanksgiving in mid-October. We talked the week before, and I asked what she wanted to do, besides eat turkey. She said she wanted me to take her, Gladys, and Elizabeth out on the water.

That was the moment she dropped the bomb. She would be bringing a friend home for the weekend. By 'friend,' she meant boyfriend. His name was Sean, and he was an engineering student at Dal.

It was never easy for me to meet one of my stepdaughter's gentleman callers, not that there had been that many of them. By definition, she was a brainy high achiever, and for the most part, didn't have time for boys. When she did bring someone home, I couldn't help but judge everything about him in the first ten seconds. Thankfully her previous boyfriends had all been good kids who cared about school. They were nothing like me when I was that age, or like any of the crowd I hung out with.

"How did you meet him?" I asked, shifting my cell phone from one ear to the other as I walked out of the clinic.

"On the dance floor at a bar on Argyle Street," she confessed.

My fatherly hackles immediately rose up.

"But he's really smart," she quickly added. "He has a giant scholarship."

I unlocked the Jeep and climbed in. "That's impressive." It was a sincere effort on my part to remain positive and open minded.

"He switched from the University of British Columbia, so this is his first time east."

"I'll look forward to meeting him," I said, wondering why he had switched. Did he flunk out? No, she mentioned he had a scholarship. "Do you need me to come get you?"

"No, Sean has a car. We'll be there Friday afternoon. Can we take the boat out to watch the sunset?"

"Sure," I said. "We're closing the clinic at noon that day, so that'll work out fine."

"Make sure Gram and Elizabeth come, too," she said. "I can't wait to see them. How is Gram, by the way?"

"She's great, honey, but..." I paused. "There have been some developments since you left. I didn't want to mention that before."

"Like what?"

I inserted the keys in the ignition, but didn't start the Jeep. I leaned my head back on the seat. "More frequent incidents of memory loss," I explained. "And some mood swings."

"Oh." I heard the disappointment in her voice and wished there was a better way to prepare her. It was going to be tough, no matter what.

"But she can't wait to see you," I said, "and I'm looking forward to meeting Sean."

"He's looking forward to meeting you, too," she replied, still sounding subdued.

We hung up, and I had a strange, uncertain feeling in my stomach.

Sean.

With a scholarship.

Engineering.

As I started the Jeep and backed out of the parking lot, I wondered how serious they were, and what kind of impression this young man would make on us.

Fifty-two

⸙

Instead of coming straight home, Marissa and Sean went to eat a late lunch at The Rope Loft, a waterside pub in town. We arranged to meet up at the marina where I kept my boat, and by the time they arrived, I had already buckled Gladys and Elizabeth into their life vests and was growing impatient.

"Hello!" Marissa called out, running along the dock.

"Hey!" I stepped out of the boat and jogged to greet her. She squeezed me in a tight hug and introduced me to her friend. "Ryan, this is Sean. Sean…Ryan."

We shook hands. "Nice to meet you," I said.

We made small talk for a few minutes. 'Where are you from?' 'Have you ever been boating before?' 'Marissa tells me you're a doctor.' That sort of thing.

"Gram!" Marissa ran the rest of the way along the dock and hopped into the boat. "I missed you so much!" She wrapped her arms around Gladys's neck and they rocked back and forth, hugging each other – though I wasn't a hundred percent sure Gladys knew who Marissa was.

"We have to wear life jackets?" Sean asked as he stepped onto the clean white boat deck.

Marissa dropped her backpack onto the driver's seat. "I told you, Ryan's a doctor. He's dealt with casualties from just about any kind of accident you can imagine. No risk-taking in our house. Besides it's the law."

"He's right about the life jackets," Elizabeth said. "If only the rest of the world could be so sensible."

I glanced at her with quiet appreciation.

"Got it. No problem." Sean held a hand up in surrender. He slipped his arms into the sleeve holes of the orange vest I held out to him, but he didn't buckle it.

As I moved to the driver's seat, I leaned close to speak quietly in Marissa's ear. "Make sure he buckles that, will you?"

"Sure," she replied, and went to take care of it.

A few minutes later we were cruising past the other boats in the marina, heading out onto the Bay.

The sunset that night turned the whole world a bright, fiery orange, and made me feel as if there could be no moment more perfect than this.

The calm water shone brightly beneath the sun's reflection, and I was able to sit back and relax on the bench while Marissa took the wheel. I moved to the bench to sit with Elizabeth and Gladys.

"What do you think?" Elizabeth asked, leaning close to me. "Does he pass muster?"

I chuckled and turned to face her. "I haven't decided yet. What do *you* think?"

"Tough call. He's good looking. That's a given, and sure, he has a big fat scholarship…but can he cook?"

I threw my head back and laughed. "We'll have to compare notes after this weekend."

"Definitely."

I don't know what came over me, but it felt completely natural to lay my hand on her knee and give it a rub. She seemed startled at first, but I didn't take my hand away. Then she met my gaze, and there was a smile in her eyes that told me she welcomed this.

I regarded her with warmth and affection, and something wonderful passed between us. My heart began to beat like a drum. The luminous orange light in the sky reflected the auburn highlights in her hair, which had grown out a few inches since the day she came to us. She no longer looked like a punk rocker. There was something soft and feminine about her now.

Most noticeable to me, her lips were full and inviting, but we were in the company of others, so I had no intention of taking any liberties.

But it was definitely cause for reflection. My wife had been gone more than two years, and this was the first time I had experienced any sort of real attraction. I had felt many things for Elizabeth since she came to us — gratitude, respect, friendship, admiration. Now desire entered the picture.

I was overcome suddenly by a confusing mixture of guilt, joy, and hope.

She continued to stare at me in the flame-red glow of the setting sun, while the hull of the boat cut lightly through the water's clear surface.

I knew in that moment that she felt what I felt. My pulse thrummed with excitement. My blood caught fire.

Hair flying in the sea breezes, Marissa turned around. "Should we head back now?"

I pulled my hand from Elizabeth's knee. "Yeah, we probably should."

Marissa stared at us for a moment, and I knew she had seen something. I saw it in her eyes. She knew me too well.

Did she disapprove?

I felt another wave of guilt, as if I were cheating on Abigail. I looked out at the water, while Elizabeth turned her face away from me and struck up a conversation with Gladys.

The thrill was smothered as Marissa took us back to the marina and slipped the boat easily into our regular spot at the dock.

I hopped out to tie the lines. She glanced at me and raised an eyebrow. I still couldn't tell what she was thinking, and maybe I should have wanted to crawl under a rock. But I didn't. All I could think about was the image of those soft, moist cherry lips on the woman in the back of my boat, and the welcoming expression in Elizabeth's eyes when I laid my hand on her knee.

For as long as I had known Gladys, she loved being out on the water, and she usually took the wheel for a good portion of our outings. I used to call her our speed demon.

Tonight, however, she had sat meekly on the bench and asked the same question over and over: "Where are we going?"

"Just for a ride, Gram," Marissa told her.

Two minutes later, she would ask the same question again, always with concern. "Where are we going?"

"Just for a ride, Gram," Marissa told her again, smiling.

When we returned to the house with grocery bags full of steaks and pre-made salads, Gladys felt tired and wanted to take a nap, so Elizabeth helped her to bed.

"There's definitely a difference since I left," Marissa said to me as we unpacked the groceries. "Tonight, I wasn't always sure she knew who I was."

"It happens a lot," I told her. "This past week, when Elizabeth was giving her a bath, she asked if she was her mother. And she's asked me, a few times, if I'm her brother or father."

Marissa closed her eyes and shook her head. "I hate being away from her. And you."

"I know," I replied, "but we're doing fine, sweetheart. Don't worry about us."

She ripped the plastic from the Styrofoam packaging and laid the steaks out on a platter. "It's been three years since the diagnosis. Don't you think it's progressing kind of fast all of a sudden? I thought we'd have more time with her."

"Every patient is different," I said, "and it's hard to say how long this was going on before she was diagnosed. She was probably dealing with it, and hiding her symptoms, for quite some time before we knew anything about it."

Elizabeth came up the stairs and turned on the baby monitor. "She's in bed. I'm not sure if she'll be up again to have supper with us. She seemed pretty exhausted."

Marissa turned away from the steaks on the counter and walked straight into Elizabeth's arms. "Thank you so much for everything you do. I don't know how we could live without you. Please don't ever leave."

Elizabeth held Marissa close and stroked her hair. Then her eyes lifted, and we locked gazes. I was completely enraptured, like an adolescent schoolboy, lost in the depths of her kindness.

Then Sean walked in with a six-pack of beer, set it down on the center island, and the spell was broken as Marissa backed out of Elizabeth's arms.

—⟳—

"Care for a brewski, Dr. Hamilton?" Sean asked as he twisted the cap off a bottle of Alexander Keith's.

"Call me Ryan," I said, "and none for me, thanks."

"Ryan doesn't drink," Marissa casually explained as she returned to the counter to sprinkle garlic powder on the steaks.

"Oh," Sean replied. He set his beer down on the island. "Should I get rid of this?"

"Don't be silly. Fill your boots," I said. "It's just not my thing, that's all."

I was acutely aware of Elizabeth moving around the island, paying close attention to the conversation. She opened a bag of baby carrots and poured them into a bowl.

Marissa picked up the steak platter and faced Sean. "Ryan had a bad experience with alcohol when he was young. He hasn't touched it since."

"Really? What happened?" Sean asked.

"I was in a car accident with some friends," I told him.

"Geez, that's rough."

"Yeah." I said nothing for a moment, and it felt awkward. "I have nothing against people drinking responsibly," I added. "It's just not for me. Leaves a bad taste in my mouth, if you know what I mean."

Elizabeth pried opened the plastic lid on a bowl of ranch dip and placed it with the carrots on the center island. "I didn't know about that," she said with her usual sensitivity. "You never mentioned it."

"It was a long time ago," I replied. "I thought maybe Marissa might have told you."

"No, she didn't."

"What happened?" Sean asked. "If you don't mind the question."

I flicked on the deck lights for Marissa, and opened the sliding glass door so she could take the steaks out to the barbeque.

"I was sixteen," I told Sean. "Two friends and I were on our way to a party in the middle of nowhere, and we were drinking. I was in the back seat, and my buddy in the front seat decided to stand up and stick his head out the sunroof. A racoon crossed the road in front of us and the girl who was driving lost control and crashed the car."

"Was anyone hurt?" Sean asked.

I hadn't talked about it in years, and felt a churning sensation in my stomach. I also felt Elizabeth's eyes trained on me with concern, so I inhaled deeply and forced the words out. "The girl who was driving was killed, and my friend flew out through the sunroof. He had brain damage and was paralyzed from the neck down."

"But *you* were okay," Sean asked.

"Yeah," I replied. "By some miracle, I came out of it with only a few scratches and a mild concussion."

Elizabeth continued to watch me with those intense eyes, and somehow I knew there were events in her own life she hadn't shared with me either, but that she wanted to. It grew quiet in the kitchen, except for the sound of Marissa outside, scraping the grill with the wire brush.

"I think I'll go see if Marissa needs any help," Sean said.

He moved past me toward the sliding glass doors, though he seemed rather invisible to me at that moment.

"I don't drink either," Elizabeth said when he slid the door shut behind him.

"I've noticed that," I replied.

I had often wondered if she was a recovering alcoholic, but it wasn't my place to ask.

"There was someone in my life who had a problem," she explained, "so like you, it always leaves a bad taste in my mouth. I just don't have any interest."

The sliding door opened again. "Do we have any barbeque sauce?" Marissa asked. "Sean wants some."

"On his *steak?*" Elizabeth and I both replied in perfect unison.

"I know, it's weird," Marissa said. "He also puts ketchup on his Kraft Dinner. And I had to teach him to eat lobster out of the shell." She came inside, fetched the barbeque sauce out of the fridge, and returned to the deck.

"I guess that answers *that* question," Elizabeth said.

I felt my brow furrow. "What question?"

She shook her head decisively. "He can't cook."

I smiled and squeezed her shoulder as I went to prepare the salads.

CHAPTER

Fifty-four

◦⟨⟨⟩⟩◦

Elizabeth took Saturday off as she always did, and I spent time with Marissa, Sean, and Gladys. We took Route 333 to the lighthouse at Peggy's Cove, which was a first for Sean, as he was from out west.

We got out of the Jeep to explore the rocky shore at the base of the lighthouse. I stuck to Gladys like glue, because the wind off the Atlantic was gusting fiercely. The surf exploded like bursts of thunder on the rocks. It wasn't the safest place for her to go wandering off.

Early in the afternoon, we ate lunch at the Sou'Wester Restaurant, then checked out a few antique shops, and returned home in time to cook some pasta, relax, and watch a movie.

It was a good day, but I missed Elizabeth. I thought of her constantly, wished she could be with us, and looked forward to tomorrow's Thanksgiving dinner, for she had promised to come and join us.

⟨⟩

Marissa rose early to stuff the turkey, which she roasted slowly in the oven for hours, basting it regularly with its glistening amber juices. By noon, the delectable aroma of the turkey – with hints of savory, onion, and thyme – filled the house with delicious splendor, and I set out to begin peeling the potatoes.

Weather-wise, it was a perfect day to celebrate Thanksgiving. The sun floated against the blue sky like a shiny gold ball, and the air was warm and still. Autumn leaves, in different shades of crimson, yellow, and orange, colored the trees around the house and the ridge on the far side of the Bay.

Elizabeth arrived at 3:00 with a homemade apple pie and a carton of French vanilla ice cream. She wore a narrow denim skirt with a hand-knit, oversized sweater, and my heart nearly beat out of my chest at the sight of her. I took the pie and ice cream from her hands, and told her about our trip to Peggy's Cove the previous day.

"Sounds amazing," she said. "I wish I could have been there with you."

I wished that, too.

Marissa set the table with Gladys's fine crystal and special-occasion china, and the five of us all sat down to gobble up the feast before us.

"That was delicious," Sean said an hour later. He leaned back in his chair to stretch his arms over his head. "Want to take a walk on the beach?" he asked Marissa.

The sun was just setting, and we had all finished our desserts and coffee.

"Sure," she replied, "but let's clear the table first."

"No, you guys go ahead," I said to them. "I'll handle it."

"I'll help," Elizabeth said.

"I'll help, too," Gladys added.

Were we all playing matchmaker now? I wondered with an easy feeling of contentment. Sean had been a perfect gentleman all weekend, polite and respectful. We had spent a lot of time together, he and I, and I couldn't help but approve of him. He was surprisingly intelligent and witty, spoke of his mother with genuine affection, and helped me figure out how to get Netflix on my phone. He handled Gladys with kindness – and humor, when it was called for – which was the icing on the cake as far as I was concerned. Sure, he had a lot to learn about the finer points of east coast cuisine, but if that was the worst of his faults, he was a fine match for my stepdaughter.

We watched them go out onto the deck and disappear down the stairs to the backyard and beach beyond. I sighed heavily, and picked up the thermos of coffee to refill my cup. "Anyone else?"

"I'll have a bit more," Elizabeth said, sliding her cup closer.

I poured the coffee, and we each added milk.

For the next few minutes, I filled Elizabeth in about Sean, and how he and Marissa were getting along. Then we all worked to clear the table and wash the dishes.

It was a good day for Gladys. Even when she was unsure about where she was or who we were, she appeared cheerful and comfortable, eager to help tidy up and do chores that were familiar to her.

Elizabeth took her to bed early, then came back upstairs. "She's out like a light. And she seemed really happy."

"I'm glad," I replied, flicking the switch on the baby monitor. "She was good today, don't you think?"

"She was great. Truly, Ryan, you're doing a wonderful job here. You're taking care of everyone so well."

"I'm not doing it alone," I reminded her.

She regarded me fondly. "We're a good team."

"Yes." I peered out the dark windows and focused on the lights on the far side of the Bay. "I wonder what the young ones are up to. I should have given them a flashlight."

"It's a full moon," she said. "I'm sure they'll be fine."

Feeling relaxed, I opened the sliding glass doors to step onto the deck. Elizabeth followed me, and together we leaned against the rail and gazed out over the moonlit water.

"What a gorgeous night," she said.

"It's times like these," I replied, "that I feel very grateful."

"For what?"

"A lot of things. It's strange. Even though my mother-in-law has Alzheimer's, and I had to bury my wife not long ago, I look out at the water on a night like this, breathe in the salty scent of the air, think of Marissa – *and you* – and I feel in awe of everything. My existence especially, because there was a time when I didn't care if I lived or died."

Elizabeth leaned her forearms on the railing and wove her fingers together. "I believe that if you've been through hell and you come out the other side, you appreciate the little things more. A night like this definitely qualifies." She looked up at the stars.

I was spellbound by her profile and the tousled curls of her hair. It had grown out quite a bit since she first arrived, and I could see red highlights.

"I wish I knew more about you," I said, feeling a strong need to pour out my soul to her, to let her know how I felt. "I want to know what sort of hell *you've* been through, Elizabeth. Will you tell me?"

Her eyes met mine and she turned around to look at the house. "I was married once," she said with a sigh, "but it wasn't good. My husband had problems. First it was alcohol, then pot, and eventually cocaine and heroin. He was involved with some bad people."

"Is that why you left him?" I asked.

Was she divorced? I wondered. Or was he abusive and was she on the run from him? Is that why she was so secretive?

"I didn't leave him," she told me. "He died."

"Oh. I'm sorry."

She shook her head and faced the water again. "It's not something I like to talk about. For one thing, it doesn't help my employment prospects if people know I was married to a drug addict. Yet, here I am, confessing my sordid past to my boss."

"I'm not only your boss," I said. "Please don't think of me just that way."

"But you sign my paychecks."

A ship's bell rang in the distance. I turned toward the water.

"I'm sorry," she said to me. "That was uncalled for. You're right. You're more than my boss. You're my friend, and I hope I'm yours. I love Gladys like my own mother, and Marissa...she's like a daughter to me. You've all made me feel like a part of this family, Ryan, and I love you for that. It's been the best year of my life."

My gaze darted to meet hers, and she blinked a few times. "Oh, that's not what I meant," she quickly added. "I didn't mean to suggest that I love you like *that*. I just...You know what I mean."

I straightened. "I do."

Sparks erupted and flew between us like a firestorm of crazy. Before I could think rationally, I pulled her toward me and slid my hand around her waist.

My mouth covered hers in a hungry kiss that pummeled all my senses. I felt the shock of it straight down to my toes.

She responded with an equal dose of passion, parting her lips and cupping my face in her hands. I steered us together, locked in the embrace, toward the shadows at the side of the house, where I backed her up against the cedar shakes and anchored her body.

She moaned with pleasure and gripped my shirt in her fists. Her hands roamed up and down my arms and over my shoulders. My heart drummed wildly. I wanted her with a fierce, unstoppable passion as I pressed my body to hers.

After a long, deep, and immensely pleasurable kiss, I eased back until our mouths were only lightly touching, and whispered, "I'm a very bad boss."

"No," she breathlessly replied. "I think you're very good."

I cupped her cheek in my hand and kissed her again, less hurried this time, more gently. Her lips were soft and moist. She tasted of coffee and sweet apple pie.

Sexual need streaked down to my core, and I had to work hard to rein in my desires, even while I was celebrating them, for it had been so long since I'd had any interest in touching a woman.

And Elizabeth was not just any woman. I felt a connection to her that went beyond physical. I cared for her deeply and I wanted to keep her here, safe with me, well loved. I wanted to share everything with her, never lose her.

I felt her ribcage expand with a deep intake of breath. Her breasts squeezed against my chest, and it was all I could do to keep from sliding my hand up under her sweater. I wanted to take her straight to bed and make love to her quick and hard, but at the same time, that was *not* what I wanted.

"My head is spinning," she whispered, as I dragged my lips across her cheek to her ear, and breathed softly into it.

Her body shuddered in response.

"Mine is, too," I replied. "You're so beautiful. I don't want to let go of you."

Wrapping her arms around my neck, she clung to me as if we were about to be violently ripped apart. I squeezed her against me and kissed her neck.

"What's happening here?" she murmured in my ear.

"I don't know," I said, refusing to release her, "but whatever it is, it's important."

It was a strange thing to say, and at the time, I had no notion of the significance of those words, but they would make sense to me later.

Marissa's and Sean's laughter and their footsteps tramping up the wooden stairs from the beach caused us to step apart. Elizabeth straightened her sweater and smoothed her hair, while I backed away from her, toward the railing.

She smiled at me, flirtatiously, and I wanted to go running down to the beach to shout across the water and tell the whole damn world that I was in love.

"Sorry we took so long!" Marissa shouted from the lawn down below. "Were you worried?"

I leaned over the railing. "Lucky for you the tide is out, young lady, or we might have sent for a rescue team."

Marissa and Sean climbed the steps. "What have you guys been up to?" she asked.

"Nothing," Elizabeth and I answered guiltily, in unison.

We looked at each other and laughed.

"Hah, hah." Marissa wagged a finger at us. "You two ought to take that hilarious show on the road."

She behaved as if nothing was amiss, but I knew Marissa sensed something as she led Sean into the kitchen. Elizabeth and I followed.

"Want to watch Conan O'Brian?" she suggested. "I notice you've been recording all his shows since I left."

"Sure," I replied. "Can you stay?" I asked Elizabeth.

"I don't have anywhere else to go," she casually replied, and we all filed into the living room.

I sat down on the sofa with a surprising sense of wellbeing, and wondered how I was going to explain to Marissa that I had fallen in love with the home care worker I had wanted to fire on the first day.

A woman who had worn combat boots and a temporary butterfly tattoo on her wrist.

Would wonders never cease?

CHAPTER

Fifty-five

⤶⤷

"There's something going on between you two, isn't there?"
Marissa asked me the following morning at the table over
breakfast.

Sean was still asleep in the spare bedroom, and Gladys was up
early as always, sipping tea with us.

"What do you mean?" I replied.

"You and Elizabeth," she clarified. "It was weird when we
came back from our walk. You missed it Gram, but they were
both blushing."

"They're such a lovely couple," she replied. "Do you have children?" she asked me.

"No, Gladys," I replied. "No kids yet, but I promise to keep
you posted."

Marissa leaned back in her chair and pointed her spoon at
me. "There. You see? I was right. There *is* something going on."

"I'm not admitting anything," I said, crunching fast on my
granola, "but hypothetically speaking, if there *was* something
going on, how would you feel about that?"

The corner of her mouth curled up in a grin. "I wouldn't have
a problem with it, Ryan. You know how I feel about Elizabeth.
For a long time I've wondered if, maybe, you're meant to be with
her. Maybe that's why she was placed in our path."

"Placed in our path," I said. "That sounds very New Age."

"Don't you believe in fate?"

"I don't know," I said.

Marissa leaned forward and rested her elbows on the table. "What *do* you believe in? Love, I hope. I also hope you're going to tell me what happened last night."

I smiled and set down my spoon. "You were always such a sucker for good gossip."

"Yes, and not much has changed."

"I like gossip, too," Gladys added, and leaned forward in her chair to hear me admit that I lost my head under the stars, and kissed Elizabeth for the first time.

And it was awesome.

— ❧ —

Marissa and Sean returned to Halifax on Monday afternoon, leaving Elizabeth and me behind to figure out our feelings for each other.

Gladys thought we were married anyway, so it seemed quite natural for us to sit together on the sofa in the evenings and hold hands. It gave Gladys pleasure to see us together – who knew she was such a romantic? – and who was I to deny an old woman such happiness?

For twenty-one days straight, we kissed at every possible opportunity. Then, late one night, after Gladys was asleep and we were making out like hormonal teenagers on the sofa, I asked Elizabeth to stay the night.

She said yes.

I woke the next morning to find her in one of my hockey jerseys, standing at the stove, cooking eggs. But Elizabeth, barefoot in my home at sunrise, was not the most notable thing. It took me a moment or two to register what was different, but I soon realized there was no sign of the butterfly on her wrist.

I felt certain that my future was sealed, and that this was why she had come to Nova Scotia.

Because she was meant to be with me.

I wish I could say it was as simple as that, but I still had much to learn about the power of destiny.

Changes

❦

Marissa

I knew, when I returned home for Christmas, that my world would be altered.

Since Thanksgiving, Ryan kept me informed about Gram's condition with in-depth phone calls every Sunday. He explained that she was declining more rapidly than expected, and he wasn't sure how much longer she'd be able to remain at home. She was no longer the woman we once knew. She couldn't remember any of our names, and sometimes she wouldn't speak for hours on end. She would just stare blankly out through the frosty windows at the fishing boats on the Bay.

Other times, when she tried to speak, she couldn't find the right words: 'I'm hungry. Can I have some dishes?' Once, she asked Elizabeth to tie her envelope.

Ryan also confided in me about his relationship with Elizabeth. He told me that she stayed over most nights, but that she was still keeping her apartment, at least for now. Not that she had much choice. Ryan had signed a one-year lease.

I was curious about their plans for the future. How serious were they? Would they get married one day? Or was this a temporary affair, meant to distract Ryan from the grief of losing Gladys, and Mom, and me?

These were questions I hoped to answer when I returned for the holidays – so I came home equipped to ask all of them.

❝I t's so good to see you," I said to Elizabeth as I crossed the
threshold and stepped into her arms. It felt like heaven to
hug her. Gram had been right. She was like a guardian
angel, sent here to care for all of us.

I noticed her hair had grown almost to her shoulders. It wasn't
as black as it was when she first arrived. There were red highlights
now, but most importantly – as Ryan mentioned on the phone –
the butterfly tattoo was gone.

"Come on in," Elizabeth said. "Let me take your jacket."

I shrugged out of it and removed my scarf, and she hung
everything up in the front hall closet.

Ryan appeared at the door and kicked the snow off his boots
before stepping inside. "The temperature's dropping," he said,
pulling off his leather gloves.

"I'm glad you made it home before dark," Elizabeth replied.

I found it interesting that she used the word home, as if it
were as much *her* home as ours. Maybe some girls my age might
have felt threatened by the presence of a potential new stepmother,
but the idea created a warm feeling in my belly, because I loved
Elizabeth. I was the one who had interviewed her, and I believed
I had made an excellent choice. I also knew Gram would not be
here forever, and I didn't want Ryan to end up alone.

"How's Sean?" Elizabeth asked, linking her arm through mine as we walked together to the kitchen.

"He's great," I replied. "His parents will be overjoyed to have him home for Christmas. He's never been so far away from them before."

"Have you met his parents yet?"

"No, but I spoke to his mom on the phone, and his little sister. She's a cutie." My gaze shifted to the living room. The television was on, but the volume was turned low. "Gram!"

I hurried around the sofa to greet her, but she peered up at me with a knitted brow. Physically, she recoiled when I went to hug her, as if I were a total stranger about to leapfrog over her.

Pausing on the area rug, I spoke more gently. "Hi, Gram. Merry Christmas."

"Merry Christmas," she replied, and I sensed she was just repeating my words. That she hadn't remembered it was the holiday season.

"What are you watching?" I asked, sitting down beside her.

She gestured toward the television. Was she having trouble accessing the words to name the program that was on?

"Mind if I watch with you?" I asked.

She nodded to tell me it was okay.

For a long while we sat in silence, then I took hold of her hand and squeezed it lovingly. She looked at me. Our eyes locked and held, and I knew she was struggling to remember who I was.

I'm not sure she ever did. She certainly couldn't form words to tell me so, but I believe in my heart that she knew I was someone who meant a great deal to her. That was enough.

On New Year's Eve, Ryan had to cover the ER at the hospital. We gave Justin the night off, so Elizabeth and I planned a special evening at home with Gram, just the three of us.

In preparation, I'd spent hours collecting old photographs from boxes in the basement, scanned them to generate digital files, and created a photo book memento using a website that allowed me to add captions and graphics. The hard copy arrived by mail a few days after Christmas, and I wrapped it in gold foil paper.

The photos I selected mostly came from Gram's childhood and the early years of her marriage, because I knew that her long-term memory was more accessible to her than what was stored in the short term. I thought Gram might recognize her sisters and parents, and be comforted by the fact that she could still remember *some* things, and that she had lived a full and wonderful life. She was not a person without a past. Without an identity. Or a soul. She was loved and valued by everyone who knew her.

Late in the afternoon, Elizabeth made a last-minute trip to the grocery store to pick up snacks and a cake we had pre-ordered to celebrate the New Year. I remained at home with Gram, who was now in the habit of wandering around the house constantly, moving from room to room, as if exploring everything for the first time. She fiddled with things, moved household items to different and sometimes bizarre locations, and often tried to go outside. We put child safety covers on all the doorknobs, which made it impossible for her to open them, and we also secured the exit doors with battery-operated alarms that Elizabeth had picked up for us at the hardware store.

I was surprised when Gram bent over the steel bucket in front of the fireplace and withdrew one of the beach rocks.

She had not painted anything since before Thanksgiving, but today she carried a sphere-shaped stone to the coffee table and set it down. She stood over it, staring for a long time.

"Would you like to paint that, Gram?" I asked, setting down the washcloth in the kitchen and moving into the living room. "We have paints and brushes." I fetched one of her other painted rocks, which we kept on the mantel, and showed it to her.

She took it from me and set it down next to the other rock.

"I'll get your paints," I said, not waiting for an answer.

After covering the coffee table with newspaper, I poured small amounts of colored craft paint from the plastic bottles onto a foil pie plate, and handed her a brush.

She dipped it into the green, mixed it with some white, and began to paint odd shapes that made no sense to me – at least not at first. But when she began to add blue, I realized she was painting a globe of the earth.

"Is that the world?" I asked, when she appeared to be finished and set down her brush.

She nodded at me.

"It's fantastic, Gram. You remember your geography better than I do." I pointed. "Look, there's Italy."

I couldn't wait to show her the photo book later that evening.

Glancing up at the clock, I wondered when Elizabeth would be back, as a light snow had begun to fall, and it was now dark.

While the paint on the beach rock dried, Gram lay down on the sofa and took a nap. I sat at the computer to watch funny animal videos on YouTube. More than a half-hour must have passed when I heard Gram mumble something. I swiveled in the chair to see if she needed anything, and noticed that the snow was coming down hard and fast outside.

Picking up my cell phone, I texted Elizabeth.

Are you on your way? It's snowing. Drive safely.

I shoved the phone into the back pocket of my jeans.

Gram sat up and stared for a long time at her painted globe. Then she stood up and walked past me.

"Do you need something, Gram?" I asked when she paused at the top of the stairs that led down to her apartment.

She pressed a hand on top of her head and winced, as if in pain.

"Are you okay?" I touched her shoulder, but she crumpled and fell forward. Down the stairs she went, tumbling fast, head over feet.

Adrenaline exploded like fire in my veins as I dashed down the stairs after her.

Gram was unconscious when I reached her. "Gram, can you hear me?" I didn't dare move her.

Though I was stricken with panic, I managed to keep my head, and with speedy hands, pulled my phone out of my back pocket and keyed in 911. "Hello. My grandmother just fell down the stairs," I told the dispatcher. "She's not conscious. Please send an ambulance."

While the dispatcher asked me questions and took my address, my heart beat like a drum, and I felt sick to my stomach. Why had this happened to Gram, and tonight of all nights, when Ryan was on call at the hospital? He would have known what to do.

And where was Elizabeth? I needed her.

I bent forward to listen for breathing, and with a profound sense of relief, found Gram's pulse at her wrist. She was alive, but I couldn't bear to think about her fall. Surely she'd done some significant damage, broken some bones – a hip, an arm, or a leg. I checked her everywhere, without moving her. There was no blood anywhere.

"Gram, can you hear me?"

Still no reply. I didn't know how long it would take for the paramedics to arrive, so I called Elizabeth's cell phone in desperation. It went straight to voicemail, which meant it was turned off, she was talking to someone, or the battery was dead.

I left a message. "Elizabeth, please come home. Gram fell down the stairs. I just called an ambulance, but they're not here yet, and I don't know what to do. She's not moving. Please call me if you get this."

I hung up and dialed Ryan's number. Thank God, he answered.

I told him what happened, and that Gram was still breathing.

"Did you call 911?" he asked.

"Yes, an ambulance is on the way."

"Is Elizabeth with you?"

"No. She went to get some groceries. Her phone is dead. What do I do? I don't know what to do."

I felt dizzy in my panic, but Ryan's steady voice helped calm me. "Don't do anything," he said. "Just stay with her and keep checking her pulse. And for God's sake, don't move her."

"I won't," I said.

"Just wait for the paramedics. They'll have the right equipment to keep her stabilized. I'll be here in the ER when she arrives, and I'll take good care of her. You did well, Marissa. I'm proud of you."

But *I* wasn't proud of me. Gram had fallen down the stairs while under my care.

I knew I would feel guilty about that for the rest of my life – there would be no escaping it.

A vehicle roared into the driveway. Hoping and praying it was the ambulance, I ran up the stairs to unlock the door.

Two male paramedics were just getting out of the cab. One hauled out a black supply bag.

It was cold and dark outside. White snow gusted off the roof. I could see my breath.

"You're going to need a stretcher," I told them, and pointed to the side of the house. "There's an entrance to the basement apartment just around that corner. It has a wheelchair ramp. I'll go unlock the door for you."

They went to fetch the stretcher, while I shut the door and ran back downstairs.

⟶⟵

As soon as the paramedics entered Gram's apartment, I backed away and gave them room to examine her. She was still breathing, but had not regained consciousness.

"My name is Gary," one of them said while he hooked her up to a heart monitor. "Can you tell me what happened?"

I explained how Gram fell, and how long ago it occurred.

The second paramedic pulled a neck brace out of the bag. He was just putting it on Gram, and they were getting ready to move her, when Elizabeth came bounding down the stairs.

"What happened?"

I felt a great sense of relief. "Thank God you're back. She fell down the stairs."

Elizabeth looked down at her. "Has she been conscious at all?"

"No," I replied. "Not since the fall. I feel terrible. It's all my fault. I was standing right next to her. She paused at the top of the stairs, then she just collapsed."

"She collapsed?"

"Yes." I shook my head, as if to clear it. "She pressed her hand to her head and winced. I touched her shoulder and asked if she was okay."

Elizabeth turned to address Gary. "What's her BP?"

"One-ninety-two over one-o-eight."

She fished through the paramedic's bag, searching for something.

"What are you doing?" Gary asked.

"Where's your pen light? Here." She pulled it out of the back, flicked it on, and checked Gram's pupils.

"Have you called Ryan?" she asked me.

"Yes, he knows we're coming."

"Call him again and tell him Gladys likely had a stroke."

"A stroke?" I replied. "Are you sure?"

Both paramedics looked at Elizabeth questioningly.

"She's not breathing," the younger one said.

"Shit," Gary said. "Let's bag and mask her."

My whole body went rigid.

Elizabeth rose to her feet and moved impatiently around the paramedics. She began pacing like a caged tiger.

"It's because of the stroke," she said. "She's got a blown pupil and the pressure on her brain is causing her to cone. You're going to have to intubate her. What's your name?"

"Gary."

She watched Gary dig into his bag and pull out a lighted scope, then he searched for the properly sized breathing tube.

"Maybe we should get her to the ambulance first," the other one said.

"Are you nuts?" Elizabeth shouted. "No, dammit; do it here!"

"He's new," Gary explained.

"*Jesus.*" Elizabeth continued to pace. Just then, the heart monitor flatlined.

Gary checked for a pulse and said, "I got nothing."

Elizabeth addressed the younger one. "Start CPR."

He leaned over Gram and began chest compressions. "Hurry up with that," she said to Gary, who was preparing to intubate.

"Ma'am – you're not helping," he curtly replied.

"Sorry." She chewed on her thumbnail, and I sensed she was fighting the urge to say more.

"Do you have epinephrine in that bag?" she asked. "Atropine?"

"Yeah," Gary said while he inserted the tube into Gram's mouth and attempted to push it down her throat.

Even I could tell he was struggling.

"It's stuck," he said, pulling it out to try again.

"Let me do it." Elizabeth knelt down and nudged him out of the way.

"Are you a doctor?" he asked.

"No."

I watched in shock as she skillfully intubated and bagged my grandmother, then told Gary to start an IV.

"Give her a milligram of epinephrine and have one of atropine ready," Elizabeth said. "Do it now."

Gary shot the drug into the IV tube while the other guy continued with chest compressions.

They transferred Gram to the stretcher and extended the wheels.

"She's not coming back," the younger one said, sounding defeated.

Elizabeth grabbed Gary's stethoscope and listened to Gram's chest. "There's no sign of pneumothorax. And her jugulars aren't distended. Let me take over." Elizabeth began chest compressions while walking alongside the stretcher as they wheeled Gram outside.

I was in shock at this point, watching in anguish as I followed them up the ramp. The frigid December wind cut through my sweater, and the snowflakes stung my cheeks like tiny razorblades. *How had Elizabeth known to do all of that?*

"I'm going to ride in the back of the ambulance with her," Elizabeth said to me over her shoulder. "Bring my car and follow us. The keys are in my purse in the front hall. Go get them, now."

I ran inside, grabbed my coat, picked up Elizabeth's purse, and hurried back outside. I locked the door behind me.

Gram was now inside the ambulance. The younger paramedic slammed the back doors and hurried around to the front. I was relieved to see that he would be doing the driving while Gary and Elizabeth would take care of Gram – because Elizabeth seemed to be the only one who knew what she was doing.

First, however, we had to get through this storm and reach the hospital. In good weather, it was a half-hour drive.

Elizabeth brought Gram back to life shortly after they backed out of our driveway, but I was not informed of that until we reached the hospital, which meant I had to endure a lonely, white-knuckled, tearful drive over snow-covered roads behind the ambulance.

I couldn't get it out of my head – how Elizabeth had pushed the senior paramedic aside and intubated my grandmother, as if she were a seasoned ER doc.

That was the moment I knew she was no ordinary home care worker. There were things she had not revealed to us on her resume, things she had kept hidden from us.

When we reached the hospital, I was told Gram was alive. Then Ryan took charge, and Gram was wheeled into the trauma room.

A short while later, a CT scan revealed that Elizabeth's early diagnosis had been correct. Gram had suffered a massive bleed in the brain while standing at the top of the stairs.

In addition, she had broken her wrist, ankle, leg, and hip in the fall.

The doctors and nurses reset her wrist and ankle with casts that night and put her in traction, but the surgery required to fix her hip would have to wait.

While Ryan worked on Gram, Elizabeth spoke with the paramedics in a back room somewhere. I was stuck in the waiting area.

When Elizabeth finally appeared, she shook hands with Gary in front of the triage room and thanked him for everything.

She approached me with a look of concern, and I felt as if I didn't know her at all. *Who was she?* Clearly, not the person I initially believed her to be. I didn't understand why she would keep something like this secret from us, yet I was eternally grateful for everything she had done for Gram back at the house.

I rose from my chair.

"Please sit," Elizabeth said as she reached me.

I didn't know what to say. This was all so strange, and I was still traumatized by the memory of Gram tumbling down the stairs.

"How is she doing now?" Elizabeth asked. "Have you heard anything?"

I shook my head. "As far as I know, she's still unconscious."

Elizabeth rubbed a comforting hand up and down my back. "It's a good thing you were there with her when it happened."

"Really?" I pinched the bridge of my nose. "That's not how I see it. I was standing right next to her, but she just...slipped out of my grasp. There was nothing I could do but watch her fall. I can't tell you how horrible it was."

There was no escaping the tears at that point.

"It wasn't your fault," Elizabeth said. "Gladys had a massive stroke. Even without the fall, she'd still be in a coma right now."

I pulled myself together and sat back, nodding. A voice came over the speaker system, calling for a Mr. Kirkman to report to the third floor nurses' station.

"How did you know how to do everything you did?" I asked her. "You're not just a regular home care worker, are you?"

Inhaling deeply, she raked her fingers through her hair. "I used to be a paramedic," she confessed. "In another life."

"What do you mean by that?"

She looked down at her hands, now folded on her lap. "You know that I was married once…"

"Yes, Ryan told me."

"Well, my husband – my *late* husband – owed a lot of money to some bad people. After he overdosed, they came looking for me to settle his debt. I didn't have the money to pay them, so they knocked me around, gave me a black eye and three days to come up with the money, or else they were going to come back and break both my legs."

"Oh, my God. Did you go to the police?"

"Yes, but they couldn't do much except promise to keep an eye on my house. I didn't feel safe, so I left town and came here to lay low for a while."

"I can't believe it," I said. "How long ago was that?"

"It's been almost two years."

I stared at her with wide eyes. "And you still don't feel that it's safe to go back?"

She shook her head.

"Why didn't you tell us about this sooner?" I asked. "Maybe we could have helped you."

"How?" She looked away from me. "You don't understand. The dealers were after me, and they're dangerous. I didn't want to involve you in that. I didn't want to put your family in danger, too."

We sat in silence for a moment while I digested everything she had told me.

"Since I'm finally confessing the truth," she continued, "you might as well know that this isn't my real hair color. And do you remember how I was dressed when you hired me? The combat boots aren't my usual style."

"The tattoo on your wrist?"

"Temporary. I quit wearing it when I began to feel like a part of your family. There were times when it seemed like that other part of my life didn't even exist anymore. I was so happy." Her eyes met mine with a meaningful stare. "And my name isn't Elizabeth. It's Kate. Kate Worthington."

I felt my eyebrows pull together in a frown. "Were you into drugs, too? I'm sorry; I have to ask."

"No. Never. It was only my husband."

I dropped my gaze. "I really wish you had told us."

"I couldn't. I was scared, and I didn't know if I could trust you. When I started to fall in love – with all three of you – I was so afraid you'd be angry, or you wouldn't trust me with Gladys. Honestly, I was going to tell you eventually. I just didn't know when, or how."

"We would have understood."

"I'm sure you would have." She looked down, as if ashamed. "I should have told you."

I glanced up to see Ryan walking toward us, pale and exhausted.

"How is she?" Kate asked.

*Kate…*It seemed strange to call her that.

He sank into the chair next to me and rubbed a hand over his face, then pulled me close to kiss my temple. "It was rough on you, baby," he said. "I'm so sorry. But you did great. So did you," he said to Kate.

I hugged him tightly. "Has she woken up yet?"

Kate leaned forward to hear his answer.

"No. We reduced the fractures in her leg and ankle and casted them, but she hasn't regained consciousness." He paused and took hold of my hand. "This isn't easy to say, Marissa, but you're going to have to prepare yourself. It was a very bad stroke. She may never wake up."

"But miracles do happen," I argued. "Surely there's a chance."

He wiped my wet cheek with the pad of his thumb. "No, honey. I'm sorry. There's too much damage in her brain."

"Was some of that damage caused by her fall?" I asked. I couldn't seem to let go of the idea that I could have prevented this, if only I had grabbed hold of her arm and pulled her one step back from the stairs, or if I had asked her what she wanted from her apartment and gone to fetch it myself.

"No, it was from the stroke," he replied.

"Can I see her?" I asked.

"Yes, but she's hooked up to a lot of machines. It won't be easy." He stood up. "You should come too," he said to Kate.

She hesitated. "Maybe you two should go in alone. I'll wait here for a bit, but then I'd like to talk to you, Ryan. In private."

"All right," he said, bewildered.

I followed him out of the waiting room.

CHAPTER

Sixty-one

The wind howled and the snow fell doggedly through the night while I sat at Gram's bedside.

Kate joined me eventually, after she confessed all her secrets to Ryan and told him her real name. They were locked away in his office for a long time. How had he taken the news? I wondered, as I waited at Gram's side. It hadn't been easy for him to open his heart to Elizabeth Jackson, but now we both had to face the fact that she wasn't who we thought she was. I felt as if everything was slipping away.

At dawn, when Ryan suggested we go home and get some rest, the storm had finally stopped raging and the sun broke through, reflecting off the clean white landscape in a blinding sea of sparkling ice crystals.

Kate and I drove home in weary silence, on roads freshly plowed and salted, while Ryan remained behind, waiting for one of the other doctors to take over his shift.

I was physically and emotionally exhausted. It was only when we pulled into our driveway – our wheels churning through a foot of tightly packed snow – that I realized it was New Year's Day.

Ordinarily, I would feel hopeful about an ambitious New Year's resolution I had set the night before, but on that bright, sunny morning, all my hopes were crushed. I couldn't seem to dig myself out of the black hole of my grief and guilt. The vision of Gram collapsing before me and tumbling down the stairs replayed over and over in my mind. I had to squeeze my eyes shut and fight hard, mentally, to push the image away.

Kate turned off the car and got out.

"Is there someone we can call to clear the driveway?" she asked, looking back toward the road. "I don't want Ryan to have to deal with this when he comes home."

"We have a snow blower in the shed," I told her, "but there's a neighbor up the road with a plow on his truck. I'm sure he'd do it for us."

The cold seeped through the mesh fabric of my running shoes as I trudged through the deep snow to the front door. Once inside, I immediately removed my shoes and slapped the snow from the bottom of my jeans.

Kate hung up our coats. We ambled to the kitchen at the back of the house, where I squinted into the blinding light that streamed in through the windows. During the night, the snow had drifted across the deck. It surged like an ocean wave up against the bottom of the glass doors, and froze there, in stillness.

The house was unusually quiet. There was not even the sound of a clock ticking. My gaze shifted to the coffee table in the living room, where Gram's blue and green painted globe sat on the newspapers.

I circled around the sofa and sat down to look at it. "She painted this just before the stroke," I said.

Kate sat down beside me. "It's beautiful. Look at all the details. Is that Nova Scotia?"

She reached out to pick it up, but I laid a hand on her forearm. "Please don't touch it."

Pausing to stare at me, Kate slowly sat back.

I felt numb inside. Confused and lost.

"Where were you last night?" I asked. "You were gone such a long time, and you didn't answer your phone when I called."

"I was waiting for the cake," she explained. "It wasn't ready when I got there. They had no record of the order."

"It takes about two minutes for a baker to squeeze out the words 'Happy New Year Gram' on a cake," I informed her.

"I had other shopping to do as well," she calmly explained. "You saw my list."

I let out a breath. "I just wish you had been here. Or at least answered your phone." Rising to my feet, I went into the kitchen to plug in the kettle.

"You're angry with me," she said, turning to rest an arm across the back of the sofa.

"I suppose I am," I coolly replied.

She watched me for a moment, and then joined me in the kitchen where we sat in silence for a moment.

"It wouldn't have changed anything if I had been here," she finally said. "You heard Ryan. It was a massive bleed in her brain. There wasn't anything anyone could do."

"I just wish you had been here," I repeated, knowing intellectually that she was right. She hadn't done anything wrong – at least when it came to the events of last night. My emotions, however, were less forgiving. I'd felt as if I'd been abandoned when I needed her, when she didn't answer her damn phone.

And what about all the lies?

I faced her. "Was this just some sort of fantasy life for you?" I asked. "Were you pretending to be the creative, loving person who took such good care of Gram? Was it all an act? And did you really fall in love with Ryan, or was he just part of the escape, too?"

"I was never trying to escape from *myself*," she told me. "I was only trying to escape the drug dealers my husband brought into my life. That was something I never wanted. My feelings for you, Gladys, and Ryan were always real, and completely unexpected. Please believe that."

I turned and poured hot water into my mug. My emotions were simmering, yet I knew it was my grief, my exhaustion, and my guilt that were fueling that fire. I needed to point my rage at something, lay blame somewhere else.

"How did Ryan take it when you told him?" I asked.

She sighed. "Not very well, I'm afraid. He was angry with me."

I set my mug down on the counter. "You didn't leave children behind, did you?"

"Of course not!" she shouted, then she calmed herself. "There were never any children, which was part of the problem in the first place. I think if Glenn and I had had a family, he might have felt some greater purpose in his life." She paused and considered that for a moment. "Or maybe not. Who knows what might have been?"

I watched her move around the island and take a seat on one of the stools.

"Why didn't you have kids?" I asked.

She cupped her forehead in a hand. "We tried, for years, but…I got pregnant in high school. The baby died two weeks before my due date. And there were miscarriages after that."

"Oh…" Suddenly, my anger over her not answering her cell phone at the grocery store seemed insignificant. I moved toward the island and set my mug down on the granite countertop. "I'm sorry."

Resting both elbows on the table, she raked her fingers through her hair. "I was in an ambulance accident. My sister and aunt were both killed. That's how I lost the baby. They had to do a C-section but it was too late. My dad said it was a girl."

Good God.

"Glenn and I…" Her eyes lifted. "He was my first love and the father of my baby. We got married right after high school because, after all that loss, I wanted to try and build a new life. I always felt my parents blamed me for my sister's death, and to be honest, I blamed myself. Textbook 'survivor guilt.' So I wanted to start fresh and fill the hole that was inside me, but you can't ever fill a hole like that. You have to live with it." She paused. "Glenn and I did okay at first, I suppose, considering how young we were. He went to college and got his teaching degree while I supported us. As soon as he finished school, I took courses to become a paramedic. But the whole time, we were trying to get pregnant, and it just never happened. It wasn't meant to be, I guess." She looked away, toward the windows. "He was a good guy back then. He was my best friend. What happened later with his addiction was…" She met my eyes again. "It was very unfortunate, and I will always wish I had been able to give him what he wanted."

"A child?" I asked.

She nodded.

"His happiness wasn't your responsibility," I said. "You had to deal with the grief of losing your baby, too. But you survived, and you were strong."

"It was the drugs that changed him," she told me. "I wish I could have prevented it."

"Just like I wish I could have prevented Gram from falling down the stairs."

She clasped my hand across the granite countertop, and we shared a look of understanding and sympathy for each other.

"I'm sorry I was angry with you," I said.

"And I'm sorry I didn't charge my phone. I should have been more on top of that."

I reached into my back pocket and pulled out my own phone. "Look at that. Mine's dead now, too." I held it up to show her, and felt the rest of my anger drain away. I circled around the island and wrapped my arms around her. "I'm glad you came to us," I said.

"Me, too," she whispered in my ear.

The front door opened just then, and Ryan walked in.

Though it was early in the morning, I closed the curtains in my room and went to bed for a few hours. When I woke, I found Ryan and Kate sleeping soundly in each other's arms on the sofa.

A comforting heat radiated through my body, and I was relieved to see that Ryan had forgiven her for the secrets she'd kept from us. If he had been angry with her at the hospital, there was no sign of that now. They looked peaceful and weightless.

Though I did my best not to wake them, they stirred when they heard me making breakfast. Ryan went to take a shower, while Kate and I fumbled sleepily at the counter, making toast and coffee.

We returned to the hospital that afternoon for visiting hours. I spoke to Gram in hushed tones, told her how much I loved her, and asked her to squeeze my hand if she could hear me.

The heart monitor continued to beep, but I received no response.

It wasn't a pleasant thing, but we all agreed that Ryan – who had been named Gram's next of kin after Abigail passed away – should sign a DNR form, which meant no heroic measures would be taken to save Gram's life if she took a turn for the worse.

Though how much worse it could be, I could not imagine.

Two days later, I was scheduled to return to school for the post-Christmas semester. I had no interest in leaving. I wanted to stay with my family and remain at Gram's bedside.

Ryan insisted that I go back. "She may hang on for weeks or months," he said. "Besides, she wouldn't want you to miss school. You're only forty-five minutes away. We'll call you if there is any change."

That night, after I packed my things, I stood on a chair in my closet to retrieve something from the top shelf – a gift I wanted Gram to have while I was gone. It was something she gave me when I was eleven. I found it exactly where I'd placed it after Mom died, in a blue cedar box, on a bed of silk flowers.

I planned to give it to Gram in the morning, when I said what might be my final good-bye to her.

As we were getting ready to leave for the hospital the next day, Kate strode into the kitchen and frowned.

"Where did you get this?"

She picked up Bubba – my stuffed blue teddy bear. I had just set him down on the kitchen island. She inspected his arms and legs, wiggled them back and forth, then pressed Bubba to her face to smell his belly.

"Gram gave him to me a long time ago," I explained. "Why?"

"Where did *she* get him?"

Puzzled, and more than a little concerned by the sense of urgency in Kate's tone, I shrugged. "I don't know. I was only eleven."

"This isn't right," Kate said. "I don't understand this."

"What do you mean?"

The front door opened. Ryan kicked the snow off his boots and removed his gloves. "The Jeep's cleaned off," he said. "Ready to go?"

With Bubba in her hand, Kate strode to meet him. "Where did this bear come from?" She held him up.

He glanced briefly at Bubba, then at me. "He belongs to Marissa."

I felt defensive all of a sudden. "I dug him out of my closet because I wanted Gram to have him while I'm gone."

"That's a great idea," Ryan said.

Kate lowered Bubba to her side. "I need to know where Gladys got him. Did she find him somewhere?"

"Why?" I asked.

She spoke brusquely. "Because he's *mine.*"

"There have got to be hundreds of those stuffed bears floating around in the world," Ryan argued as we stood in the front hall.

"Not like this one," Kate said. "My mother made him. She used a Butterick pattern."

Ryan's eyebrows pulled together in disbelief. "Are you sure? I mean, Marissa's had that bear for years."

"And I had him for years as well. I know he's mine. If you don't believe me, open him up. Take him apart at the side seam, and you'll find a little red heart inside. It's made of felt and stuffed with white cotton. I sewed the heart with my own hands when I was six. My mother said it would hold lots of love."

Ryan and Kate stared at each other intently, as if the same wheels were turning inside their heads.

But what wheels, exactly? I had not yet figured that out.

I grabbed Bubba out of Kate's hands. "I have a seam ripper in my room. We'll go and find out for sure."

I found my sewing kit in the bottom desk drawer, lifted it out, and flipped open the lid.

"Be careful," Kate said as I examined the side of Bubba's belly, searching for a good place to break the seam.

"Did you lose him somewhere?" Ryan asked Kate while I tugged and sliced at the threads. "Or sell him at a yard sale?"

"We didn't sell him," Kate replied. "I lost him the night of the accident when we were on our way to the hospital. My sister, Mia, brought Bubba to Boston where I was supposed to have my baby. But the accident happened, and I never saw him again."

"Someone must have found him on the road," I said as I pulled the seam apart. I felt uneasy sticking my fingers inside, so I handed Bubba to Kate. "Here, you do it. You know what you're looking for."

She took Bubba from me and gently probed the stuffing in his belly, then withdrew a tiny felt heart. It was stitched clumsily and jaggedly around the edges with white thread.

Kate sat down on my bed, closed her eyes, and hugged Bubba to her chest. "I can't believe this. I thought I lost everything that day," she said.

I sat next to her and laid a hand on her shoulder. "This is so weird. How in the world did I end up with him? What are the odds?"

She stared at me for a long moment, then looked up at Ryan. "Can I talk to you for a minute? Alone?"

"Sure," he replied. "Marissa?"

"Yeah? Oh…" I stood up. "I'll wait in the kitchen."

About ten minutes later, they both descended the stairs and asked me to join them on the sofa in the living room. "Sit down, sweetheart," Ryan said. "We need to ask you something."

"**O**f course I'm not adopted," I replied, staring at both of them in shock. "Why would you even ask that?"

"I'm sorry," Kate said. "I know it must sound strange, but you're the exact age my child would be if I didn't have that accident."

"But you *didn't* give birth," I reminded her. "You told us your baby died."

"That's what I was led to believe, but my father...I just don't know. I never saw my child's remains because I was in a coma for two weeks, and they transferred me from the Boston hospital to Bar Harbor, so he could have lied about it, changed my records somehow. I was only sixteen, and he was principal of the elementary school. I think he would have done *anything* to make the problem disappear." She set Bubba down on the coffee table. "And I've always felt like it wasn't true. I've felt like my child was out there somewhere. It's haunted me all my life."

Ryan sat forward and laid a hand on my knee. "Marissa, are you sure Abigail never mentioned anything that made you wonder? What about Gram?"

"Nothing," I replied. "And this is crazy. I agree that it's bizarre that I ended up with your teddy bear, but that's where the connection ends. I think you're grasping at straws here, wanting something that just isn't true." I turned to Ryan. "I can't believe you're even asking me this. You were married to Mom for fifteen years."

"Yes, but I didn't know her when you were born. You were very young when I married her."

"And now you believe Kate over her?" I gestured toward Kate with a hand. "Do I need to remind you that she's been lying to us, keeping things from us since the day we met her?" I looked at Kate directly. "Now I'm starting to think you might have some issues you need to deal with. I'm not trying to be cruel, but you've been through a lot."

Kate cupped her forehead in a hand. None of us spoke for a long moment.

"I shouldn't have asked you this," she said, looking up. "You're right, it is crazy." She stood. "Maybe I *am* losing my mind."

She went to pick up her purse from the chair by the computer.

"Where are you going?" Ryan asked.

"Home," she said. "I need to be alone for a bit. And I need to call my father and ask him about this."

"Wait a second…" Ryan followed her to the door. "There's a simple way to find out whether or not Marissa is your daughter. We can do a paternity test – or in this case, a maternity test. It's very simple and you'll have an answer in about a week. We can order the test online, as long as Marissa is willing."

"Of course I'm willing," I said, joining them in the front hall. "I won't go back to school today. We'll clear this up first. And I'm really sorry, Kate. I don't mean to crush your hopes. It must have been a terrible thing to lose your baby, but I really don't think I'm her."

"I'm sure you're right," she said. "I should go."

She left without kissing Ryan good-bye, and as I stood in the chill of the open doorway, watching her get into her car and back out of the driveway, I worried about her.

"Let's order that test," Ryan said, heading for the computer.

I shut the door and followed him. "You don't really think it's true, do you?"

"I have no idea," he said, "but no matter what the answer is, *she* needs to know."

Ryan and I went to the hospital that morning. While he checked out Gram's file to see how she was doing, I sat next to her bed and held her hand.

"I have something for you, Gram. Remember this?"

I laid Bubba next to her cheek and watched for some sign of a response – a twitch in her hand perhaps, a flick of her eyelids – but I saw nothing. The heart monitor continued to beep in a dreary, monotonous rhythm, and the ventilator contracted and expanded, pushing air into her fragile lungs.

Holding her thin, blue-veined hand, I rested my elbows on the cold, shiny bedrail. "I need to ask you something, and I really wish you could answer me."

Beep…beep…beep….

"Kate confessed something to us," I said. "It turns out that she got pregnant when she was sixteen…Yeah, I know. Rough, eh? But she lost the baby in an accident. It happened a few weeks before her due date, and it was very devastating for her. I felt really bad when she told me.

"But here's the strange part," I continued. "She had Bubba with her on the night of the accident, because Bubba used to be *her* teddy bear. Isn't that weird, Gram?"

Beep…beep…beep…

"Kate's mother made Bubba for her, and Kate sewed a tiny heart to put inside him. She said it was to hold lots of love. All these years, I never knew it was there, but I certainly felt the love."

I swallowed hard and took a deep breath.

"I care for Kate very much, Gram, and I don't want to lose her. Ryan cares for her, too, but I think she's very lost. At least, that's how it seems. But I need to ask you something, and I know you can't answer me, but I'm going to ask anyway." I swallowed hard and squeezed her hand. "Am I Abigail's true biological child? Or did she adopt me?"

Again, I waited for a sign – a twitch of Gram's finger, or maybe her eyes would flutter open.

Still, nothing.

A painful lump formed in my throat, and I found it difficult to breathe.

"I wish you were here, Gram," I said. "I really need to talk to you. I miss you."

I stroked her hair away from her face, and wept quietly until I felt Ryan's hand on my shoulder.

Back to the Beginning

Sixty-six

Kate Worthington

Yes. It's true.

For the past two years, I have been living a lie.

I came to Nova Scotia to escape a drug pusher who wanted money from me – money that my husband owed to him. I changed my name, took on a new identity, and found work in a nursing home.

The rest you already know. I was hired to work for a wonderful family in Chester, perhaps brought to them by fate, destiny, or God. Whatever you want to call it.

I certainly didn't know what to call it.

How many times had I looked up at the stars and prayed that my child would have all the things I never had? That she would have a perfect, magical life, like the privileged set in Bar Harbor who sailed their yachts up the coast each summer to attend Chester Race Week?

It's what drew me here to Nova Scotia two years ago – that dream of freedom and fulfilment, when I felt I had to escape from my life, before I lost it. I wanted to be like *them*.

Was it actually possible that I somehow knew where my daughter was? That my prayers had been answered, and Marissa Smith was the unborn child I had lost in that accident, twenty years earlier?

Sounds crazy, I know.

Keep reading.

⁓

If Marissa had survived the C-section while I fought for my own life after the accident, and had been given to another woman to raise as her own, there was only one person who could orchestrate such a plot...My father, Lester Worthington.

My hands shook with fear and rage as I dialed his home number in Connecticut. I doubt I need to explain why I was filled with rage, but the fear...That was more complicated.

What was I afraid of, exactly? That he would scold me for lifting the lid on a box he preferred to keep shut? Or was I afraid of the answer he would give? What if he told me it was true? That, yes, he had seized the opportunity and arranged an adoption of my baby while I was in a coma...

Or worse...what if he told me he would never do such a thing, and the baby was dead. The baby had *always* been dead.

I felt like I was pulling a trigger and firing myself like a bullet back in time to that horrific day twenty years ago, when I woke up in a hospital bed to discover that my sister and aunt had been killed, and my belly was flat; there would be no tiny infant to hold in my arms.

I wasn't sure I could bear to hear that news again. I wanted to feel joy and magic from learning that Marissa was my birth daughter.

All the while, I knew it was madness. Marissa couldn't possibly be my long-lost daughter. My life was not an afternoon soap on television. This was the real world, and I was not an emotional, irrational woman who believed in fantasies and fairy tales. To the contrary, I had never believed in miracles – not even when I watched a drowned woman from a frozen lake come back from the dead.

Carefully, I pushed the buttons to dial my father's number, and sat down at the table as soon as I heard ringing on the other end.

Click. "Hello?"

My stomach dropped. I hadn't spoken to him in over a year.

"Hi, Dad. It's Kate."

Silence.

"Are you there?" I asked.

"Yes, I'm here." His voice was low and gruff – the same as always. There was a time that voice intimidated me into obedience, but those days were long gone. The anger and disconnect I felt toward him smothered any childish trepidation.

"I'm surprised to hear from you," he said. "It's been awhile."

"Yes, it has," I replied, "but I'm doing okay." Not that he had asked. "How are you?"

Despite everything, I would at least remember how to be gracious. For the moment.

"I'm doing just fine," he said. "Where are you, Kate? Still up in Canada?"

"Yes. I think the last time we spoke I was working at the nursing home, but I left there to work with a family dealing with Alzheimer's."

"I see…Well that sounds like a noble pursuit."

Noble…Did he even know the meaning of that word? How about empathy or compassion? Loyalty? Trust?

"I think I know why you're calling," he said, and my stomach turned over.

"You do?"

"Yes. You want to know about Jack Wilbur. You must have heard the news."

Jack Wilbur was the drug dealer who had come after me a few days after I found my husband dead on my sofa.

"No, I didn't hear anything," I said. "Did something happen?"

There was a pause. "You didn't hear? He was arrested ten months ago…along with most of the people who were running his shady outfit. He was sentenced to thirty years for all kinds of crimes besides dealing drugs. But who knows when he'll get out on parole."

I blinked a few times, and absorbed this news. "Why didn't you call me?" I asked.

"I did. I left a message on your answering machine."

"I never got it. Why didn't you try my cell?"

"Look. I made the call. Don't blame me if you lost the message."

He hadn't bothered to make sure I knew about Jack Wilbur's arrest, and that it was finally safe to come home. Swallowing hard over the urge to shout at him through the phone, I struggled to focus on the reason I had called him.

"I need to ask you something," I said, "and I want you to tell me the truth."

"Sure," he replied.

I could picture him leaning back in his leather recliner, frowning with curiosity.

I wasn't certain how to begin. "Do you remember my blue teddy bear? We called him Bubba?"

"Yes."

"He was with me in the ambulance when Mia was killed. Whatever happened to him?"

Dad paused. "I don't know, Kate. I suppose he was lost in the wreckage."

"Are you sure about that?"

"No," he replied, "because I have no idea what happened to your things. Why are you asking me this?"

My heart was racing. I took a deep breath. "What happened to my baby, Dad?"

"I beg your pardon?"

I stood up and paced around the kitchen. "You said she didn't survive the accident, but I never saw her remains, and I've always felt she wasn't really gone. I need to know…Did you take her from me?"

There was a long pause on the other end. "*Take* her from you? What are you insinuating?"

"That she didn't die," I said. "I can't help but wonder if, while I was in a coma, you gave her up for adoption. We both know you wanted to get rid of her from the beginning."

"Kate!" he scolded, but I didn't let him finish.

"Black market adoptions happen all the time," I said. "There are plenty of couples willing to pay anything for a child. Is that how you were able to pay off the mortgage after the accident? Why you were able to pay for my courses when I wanted to become a paramedic? Was that guilt money?"

"Good God!" he shouted into the phone. "Are you doing drugs too?"

I covered my eyes with a hand. "No, Dad. And that was a low blow. You know I don't even drink."

"Then explain to me where this nonsense is coming from. You actually believe that I would steal your baby, tell you she died, and sell her on the black market? I think you need help, Kate. That's all I can say to you."

"Wait a second," I said desperately. "Do you know a woman named Gladys Smith? Or Abigail Smith?"

"No. Good-bye." *Click.*

Just like that, he hung up on me.

I slammed the phone down onto the charger, then buried my face in my hands. "This is insane!" I cried. "What am I doing?"

⁓

The phone in my apartment rang at about 9:00 that evening. "Hello?"

"Hi, Kate. It's Ryan."

I sat down. "Hi. It's good to hear your voice. How's Gladys doing?"

"She's the same," he replied. "Marissa and I spent the day with her, but I have to be honest, I'm not hopeful. I think Marissa is beginning to realize that this is the beginning of the end, and it's only a matter of time."

"I'm so sorry. How's Marissa holding up?"

"As well as can be expected. She's a trooper, that one."

"Yes. She's strong. You and Abigail did a great job with her."

He was quiet for a moment. "How are *you* holding up, Kate? I'm sure you have a lot on your mind."

All the tension and anger I felt earlier when I spoke to my father evaporated like mist in the sun. I crawled onto my bed and lay my head on the soft pillow.

"I'm sorry for springing this on you and Marissa now, when we should all be thinking of Gladys. I wish I could reverse that conversation we had this morning, and put it off until later."

"Sometimes things are meant to happen a certain way," he said. "And you have nothing to apologize for. Frankly, I'm still reeling from that little red heart inside of Bubba. I can't believe Marissa has had that bear most of her life, and the whole time, your heart was inside him. It's incredible."

Tears filled my eyes. I fought to keep my voice steady as I spoke. "It is kind of freaky, isn't it?"

I rolled to my side and pressed the phone up against my cheek.

"You know," he said, "even with everything that's been going on, I still feel blessed for the life we've had. Marissa does too. We were talking about that on the way home from the hospital tonight. How we wanted to remember and celebrate the wonderful life Gladys lived, and how lucky we were to have her for as long as we did."

"You're so right," I said. "She's an amazing woman."

He fell silent. "Will you still feel that way, even if it turns out that she was responsible for adopting Marissa? Won't you feel some resentment toward this family if they took part in an illegal adoption?"

"We don't know if that's true yet," I said. "I spoke to my father tonight. I came right out and asked if he lied to me and gave my baby away for adoption."

"What did he say?"

"Well, first he told me that the drug dealer who came after me was arrested ten months ago and sentenced to thirty years in prison. So it turns out I could have returned home. My dad said he left a message, but he probably left it at my old number. He didn't follow up. What kind of parent does that?"

"I'm sorry, Kate. About your dad, I mean. But I'm not sorry to hear that the drug dealer's in jail. That's good news, at least."

"Yeah, for sure."

I closed my eyes and listened to the sound of Ryan's breathing through the phone. It comforted me.

"What about the other situation?" Ryan asked. "The reason you called him? What did he say about your baby?"

I sighed. "He denied it of course – which could mean he's hiding it, or it could mean I'm nutty as a fruitcake and it never happened."

"You're not nuts," Ryan said. "It's a reasonable question, considering the fact that Marissa has Bubba, and she's exactly twenty years old."

"But her birthday is a whole month off."

"That could have been doctored on the paperwork if it was an illegal adoption. They would have wanted to wipe out the trail and hide any trace of who she really is."

I rolled onto my back and blinked up at the ceiling. "What do you think?" I asked. "Could it be true?"

He sighed. "I honestly don't know, but I have to admit, I've been staring at Marissa sometimes, trying to figure out if she looks like you. Abigail was very blonde, and Marissa has dark features. I never really thought they looked that much alike, but I never knew her father. I only saw pictures of him." Ryan paused for a moment. "The DNA test will tell us for sure. I made a few calls and was able to expedite the process. You and Marissa will have to come in to the clinic in the morning. We'll take a swab from each of you and send the samples straight back to the lab. We should have an answer in a few days."

I took a deep breath. "Wow. The miracles of modern medicine."

"Yeah," he agreed. "Listen, are you going to be okay tonight? I could come over, or you could come here."

I considered it. "I'm not sure how Marissa would feel about that. She can't be happy about all this. I basically pulled the rug out from under her whole life, suggested that the mother she worshipped might have kept this secret from her since the day she was born."

"Don't worry about Marissa," Ryan said. "She has a good head on her shoulders." He paused. "But I need to tell you, Kate…She doesn't believe it's true. She told me she was only taking the test to ease *your* mind, because she understands that you need to know."

"What do *you* believe?" I asked.

He hesitated. "After seeing that little felt heart we removed from Bubba this morning? I believe anything's possible."

CHAPTER

Sixty-seven

⁓ ❧ ⁓

I met Ryan and Marissa at the clinic the following morning. We finished the test in fifteen minutes. It all seemed so fast and straightforward. At one point, I wanted to say, "Stop. Slow down. This is important." But before I could say a word, it was done, and the samples were sealed and waiting to be picked up by the courier.

"Want to come to the hospital to visit Gram?" Marissa asked me on the way out. It took me a moment to collect my thoughts. "Ryan has patients to see here, but he said I could take the Jeep."

"Let's take my car," I suggested, focusing on the opportunity to be alone with Marissa and talk to her about the situation.

"Ryan says you're handling everything really well," I said as we pulled out of the clinic parking lot.

"He said the same thing to me about you," Marissa replied, but this time, I detected a hint of animosity in her tone.

I flicked the blinker and turned left onto the number three highway.

"I'm really sorry about this," I said. "I know it's the worst possible time to have something like this come up. I hate that it happened this way."

I felt her eyes boring into my profile as I drove along the winding road.

"Are you angry with me?" I asked.

"No," she replied. "I'm just looking at your face and comparing it to my mom's. You both have full lips and similar noses. I'm trying to figure out if I look more like you or her."

This fascinated me. "And...?"

I lightly touched the brakes and glanced briefly at Marissa. She faced forward.

"I think I look more like *her.*"

Later, when we were sitting in Gladys's room, Marissa looked at me from across the bed. "I'm sorry about what I said in the car earlier. That was insensitive."

"No need to apologize," I replied.

She studied my expression. "But this must be hard for you, to learn that your baby might have been taken from you, that you were deprived of the chance to raise her."

I wasn't sure I could describe how those events from twenty years ago had affected my life. Sometimes I wondered how I ended up childless, married to a drug addict, and estranged from my parents. An only child, when I'd once had a sister.

Then somehow I found the words.

"I lost a piece of my soul that day," I said, "and everything seemed like damage control after that. My parents blamed me for my sister's death, as if it were all my fault that she decided to visit me in Boston. Glenn, my boyfriend, was the only one who truly understood how devastated I was, and I suppose he blamed himself for my unhappiness. When he married me, he just wanted to fix everything and rescue me, be my knight in shining armor, and I can't deny that I needed one. We were only eighteen when we got married. He promised we would have more children and live the life we always dreamed about, but we just couldn't get pregnant again."

"Did you try fertility treatments?" Marissa asked.

"Yeah, we tried everything. I had three miscarriages and then…I guess we both started to believe we were cursed, and weren't even meant to be together."

"You were so young," Marissa said.

I nodded. "After he overdosed, I was a woman adrift – until I met you, Gladys, and Ryan."

A nurse came in to check Gladys's vitals. I waited until she was gone before I continued.

"If it turns out that you're my daughter," I said, "and I could change what happened to me that night, I'm not sure I would want to, because look at you now. You are exactly what I dreamed my daughter would become. You had a wonderful mother and father and the kind of life I knew I could never provide. Now, I just need to feel grateful for how my life has turned out, because no matter what happens, I feel blessed to have met you."

Marissa reached across the bed and squeezed my hand. "I feel blessed, too."

CHAPTER

Sixty-eight

❧

The Results

I was home alone in my apartment finishing breakfast when my cell phone rang.

"Hello?"

"Hi, Kate. It's Ryan. Hope I didn't wake you."

"No, I was just making some coffee."

Nervous butterflies invaded my belly, for I had been waiting five days for the test results. I had elected to have them sent to Ryan's office, since he was Marissa's legal guardian, and I suppose I wanted him to be the one to deliver the news. To both of us.

"I'm sure you know why I'm calling," he said.

"I can guess."

The coffee pot gurgled and hissed. I felt almost dizzy with anticipation, and moved slowly to a chair to sit down.

"Do you want me to open it now," he asked, "and give you the news over the phone? Or do you want me to call Marissa first, and you can come in together?"

I stood up again and paced back and forth in my kitchen while I considered both options. "Open it now," I said. "If it's something Marissa needs to know, I think you should be the one to tell her. But I can't wait any longer."

I heard the sound of the tape ripping across the courier enve-lope, then paper unfolding, followed by silence. Only a few sec-onds went by, but it felt like many minutes.

"Are you reading it?" I asked.

"Yes."

My heart pounded against my ribcage. I was sure it was going to beat right out of my chest. "What does it say?"

He paused. "Maybe I should have asked you to come in."

"Why?"

My knees went weak. I sank back down onto one of the kitchen chairs while I waited for him to tell me the result, yet somehow I knew the answer. I could hear it in his voice.

"There was a negative result, Kate," he told me. "Marissa's not your daughter. I'm sorry."

The finality of his words held me immobile. I experienced a sudden, acute sense of loss. It was so painfully familiar. A repeat of many years ago, like déjà vu.

Sitting very still, I waited for my emotions to settle.

"Are you okay?" Ryan asked.

"Yes." I took a moment to steady my voice. "Are you sur-prised? Or is this what you expected?"

"I told you before," he said, "I believed anything was possible."

Disappointment sat like a ball of lead in my stomach, and I had to steel myself against the urge to cry. "You don't think I'm a nutcase? I mean, it was such a long shot. Way out there."

"Yes, but you're way out there, too, Kate. Remember how Gladys used to say you were like a guardian angel sent to us? I've felt the same way, and it made me believe in...I don't know what...magic, or fate, or destiny. Something beyond pure dumb luck. Marissa may not be your biological daughter, but I can promise that she loves you."

Tears welled up in my eyes. "I love her, too."

As I sat there comprehending the fact that Marissa was not the living child I thought I'd lost, I tried not to fall apart, but I felt completely broken. This meant I was not a mother. I was *no one's* mother.

My baby was truly dead. She was not coming back.

I went for a walk alone that afternoon, down onto the small rocky beach near the yacht club. Clearly I *was* a nutcase, for I was the only person crazy enough to venture out into sub-zero temperatures with a wind chill that gusted off the white-capped Bay and took a sharp stinging bite out of my cheeks.

As I stood looking out at the rough gray water and sniffed in the cold, I wondered what the hell I was doing here so far away from my real life. I had become an imposter, running from my past.

Certainly, one could argue that I was running from a drug dealer who wanted me to pay my dead husband's debts, but I knew that wasn't the whole story. I had come here to the farthest corner of a country that was not my own, searching for something.

What, exactly? A way to exist in a state of denial about how my life had unfolded? To start again with a fresh, clean slate? Was that even possible? Because no one could ever truly erase the past.

Maybe there was something wrong with me. Surely a normal woman would find it difficult to allow every shred of her identity to be stripped away – her name, her profession, her community, and family. Yet here I stood, eager to remain a ghost, still hiding in so many ways from the very people who had opened their hearts to me, given me everything, trusted me with everything.

Surely I was crazy to have believed that Marissa was my long lost baby girl, returned from the dead and reunited with me by some miracle of destiny.

She wasn't my daughter, but oh, how I'd wanted her to be. When my gaze had fallen on the teddy bear from my childhood, something woke up inside of me. I felt a sense of hope I had never let myself reach for. Suddenly I believed there *could* be magic in the universe, and this was how it was all meant to be – that the baby I couldn't care for when I was sixteen had found a wonderful family, and she had been raised in a loving family with everything I wanted for her.

But Marissa was not the baby I had lost in the ambulance accident. That baby was gone, and whatever longing I felt for her over the past twenty years was not the real pull of a mother toward her lost daughter. It was grief and regret, plain and simple.

I wondered if it was ever possible for a mother to let go of a lost child, of any age.

My cell phone vibrated in my coat pocket and I jumped.

I pulled my mitten off with my teeth and fumbled to reach for it. The call display said Dr. Ryan Hamilton. I swiped my fingertip across the answer button.

"Hey," I said.

"Hi Kate," he replied. His voice was quiet and low.

A gust of icy wind blew into my face. I immediately turned my back on it. "Is everything okay?"

"Not exactly. I'm sorry to tell you this now when it's already been a rough day, but Gladys isn't doing so well. She won't likely make it through the night."

I started walking back toward the road. "I'm so sorry. Is there anything I can do?"

"Yeah," he said. "Could you come to the hospital and sit with us? Gladys would want you to be there."

I stopped for a moment. "What about Marissa?"

"She wants you there, too. She's the one who asked me to call you."

I began walking up the steep hill toward my car. "Ryan…I have to ask. Does Marissa know the results of the DNA test yet?"

"Yeah," he said, "I told her."

A dog barked at me viciously from someone's front window as I walked past their house. "She was probably relieved."

"I won't lie to you, Kate. She was, because she loved her mom a lot, but it doesn't change how she feels about you. Will you come?"

By now, I was walking at a brisk pace toward my car. "I'm already on my way."

I am no stranger to death. My experience with it began when I lost my sister, aunt, and my unborn child in an ambulance accident, and continued when I lost my husband, who had chosen to give up on life.

In addition, I had entered a profession that put me inside death's intimate circle on a daily basis, though thankfully, I saved far more lives than I lost.

There was nothing I could do to help Gladys, however, that night in the hospital. All I could do was sit quietly at her bedside with Ryan and Marissa, knowing it was time for her to go.

I only wished it was not so difficult for those of us left behind.

We lost Gladys shortly after midnight. Her heart just stopped beating and the nurse said, "She's gone." I glanced about the room, searching for something – some evidence of Gladys's spirit departing for another destination. Did heaven even exist? Was there a higher power?

But there was no rising mist, no shudder within me, no ghostly whispers of good-bye – only a profound and devastating silence that followed the sound of her last breath.

Destiny

Marissa

Do you believe in happy endings? I do. I've learned that even when life drags you down into the deepest pit of despair, that's the most important time to keep believing, because you never know when you're going to sling-shot upwards, straight out of there.

Three months after Gram passed, Ryan proposed to Kate. They were married that summer in a quiet ceremony in our backyard overlooking the water. We arranged Gram's colorful painted stones into an aisle for Kate to walk down, and rented white chairs and a tent for the afternoon.

I was Kate's maid of honor, and Ryan asked a close friend of his from medical school to be best man. His name was Jacob and he drove six hours from his practice in the Cape Breton Highlands to be there.

Sean wasn't able to attend because he had a summer job in British Columbia, and he couldn't get the time off. I hated being away from him, and though I wasn't absolutely sure, I thought Sean might be the one. Only time would tell.

When August came, I held down the fort at home while Ryan and Kate flew to Italy for their honeymoon. It was lonely without Gram, and without them. The house seemed eerily quiet, and I couldn't bring myself to open the door to Gram's apartment and look down the stairs.

Maybe that's why I tried so hard to keep busy with work, taking on extra shifts at the yacht club as it prepared for Chester Race Week.

Or maybe it was another reason entirely. Maybe it was destiny that made me a crew member on the *Gemini*, as a fill in for someone during a practice run, three days before the race.

I was asked to replace Adam Moore, the eldest adult son in a family of five. He had come down with a bad sinus infection upon his arrival in Nova Scotia and needed to rest up before the competition.

Mr. and Mrs. Moore had two daughters, Diana and Rebecca, ages twenty-three and twenty-one. The commodore of the club called me into his office to explain that the Moores were very important guests. Gerald Moore was a member of the US Senate and had been coming to Race Week with his family for the past fifteen years. They were two-time winners of the trophy. Now their children were grown and spread out across the country, but they were determined to continue the family tradition. They came together each summer, and sailed up the coast to try and win the race one more time.

When I stepped onto their clean white boat deck, I shook hands with Senator Moore and his wife, Sandra, then turned to meet his two daughters. The older one, Diana, was in law school at UCLA, and the younger one, Rebecca, had just finished a degree in classics at Princeton. In the fall she would attend Oxford University in England to do her masters. She told me to call her Becky.

After the initial introductions, the senator led me to the companionway that took me down to the cabin where I could store my backpack.

It was a luxurious boat with a well-appointed galley and shiny brass fittings everywhere. I stowed my backpack into a lower cupboard and returned to the deck where Becky and Diana were already preparing for the morning sail.

I, too, set to work with Mrs. Moore, putting the batons in the mainsail and jib. Before long, we were pulling on the sheets to hoist the sails, and moving out onto the Bay.

"Too bad Adam couldn't be here!" Senator Moore called out from the helm. "It's such a great morning!"

Becky hopped down from the foredeck to join him. She passed under the boom, then slid her arm around her father's waist and laid her head on his shoulder.

The wind was fresh and cool on my cheeks, gulls circled above, and I felt a warm glow inside myself as I watched the senator kiss his daughter on the top of her head.

Glancing up at the mainsail, I wondered how Ryan and Kate had enjoyed their honeymoon. I couldn't wait to see them. They'd been gone for two weeks, but were due back the following day. I was to pick them up at the airport shortly before noon.

Though I was the newest member of the crew, I fell into an easy rhythm with the others, following our captain's orders to adjust the lines and trim the sails when we tacked.

After the third tack, the boat heeled to starboard and we all relaxed for a while.

Becky, who was seated at the windward shrouds, her red hair blowing wildly in all directions, smiled at me. "So you go to Dal?"

"Yeah!" I shouted over the sound of the waves rushing past the hull. "I just finished a science degree."

"Have you decided what you're going to do next?"

I pushed my bangs away from my face. "I'm starting my masters this fall. I might apply to medical school after that."

"Wow," she said. "That's ambitious. Good for you. I was never very good at science."

"But you must be good with the classics," I said. "Oxford... That's ambitious, too."

She shrugged as if it wasn't that important, and I admired her humility. I'd met more than a few Ivy Leaguers at the yacht club over the years, and some of them were downright snobby.

"Does your family live in Washington?" I asked.

"My dad has an apartment there, and he and Mom live there most of the time, but our real home is in Bar Harbor, Maine. That's where I grew up."

My eyebrows flew up. "Oh! I know someone from Bar Harbor."

"Yeah? Who?"

"My stepmom. Her name is Kate Worthington. She grew up in Maine, and her father was principal of their elementary school, I think. She became a paramedic and worked in New Hampshire for a while, but now she lives here."

"Cool." Becky's face lifted, and she squinted up at the top of the mast.

I found myself staring, absorbedly, at her profile. She had a tiny upturned nose and a freckled complexion, and long, thick, wavy red hair tied back in a ponytail.

I glanced at her sister, Diana, who had olive skin, brown eyes and jet-black hair.

Then I turned my gaze to their mother, Sandra, who was standing at the stern looking ahead with a hand raised to shade her eyes from the sun. She was blonde and just as gorgeous as her daughters. She reminded me of Michelle Pfeiffer.

The senator, at the helm, was an attractive, athletic-looking gentleman with warm, smiling eyes, a strong jaw, and salt and pepper hair.

Maybe I should have put two and two together, but the number four didn't even occur to me until we returned a few hours later to the marina. We had just finished tying the lines, and had secured the boat.

The senator stepped onto the dock and waved at someone up on the lawn of the club. The man came jogging down to meet us.

"You feeling better?" the senator asked when the man arrived at the boat.

By that time, I was slinging my backpack over my shoulder and joining the senator on the dock.

"Marissa," he said, "I'd like you to meet my son. This is Adam."

Slightly surprised, I reached out to shake Adam's hand. "It's very nice to meet you."

I was surprised because Adam Moore was African-American.

That night, I pulled the Jeep into the driveway, went straight inside, and Googled Senator Moore and his children. It took me awhile, because there were dozens of articles and pictures of the family at political and social events all over the country.

Then *wham*. I found it. The in-depth article I was searching for.

I leaned forward in my chair to read about the famous Moore family from Bar Harbor. Theirs was a rags-to-riches story. Senator Moore had grown up in poverty with a single, but loving and devoted mother.

On the day he and Mrs. Moore were married, she wore a wedding gown she'd purchased at a second hand store, and they went camping for their honeymoon.

They spent the first few years of their marriage building schools in third-world countries, which was how they ended up with their first son, Adam. As soon as they returned to America, Mr. Moore dove into a career in public service, and rose quickly in political circles.

As for his family life...It was just as I suspected. For reasons that were not disclosed in the article, the Moores were not able to have a family of their own.

All the senator's children were adopted.

I drove to the airport the following day to meet Ryan and Kate, who had taken the red eye from Rome to Toronto, which meant they didn't have to go through customs when they arrived in Halifax. For that reason, they reached the baggage carousel not long after touching down.

I hugged them both and asked about their trip. They described the food and the culture and the mind-blowing ancient ruins, and told me I had to travel to Europe as soon as I could manage it.

We collected their suitcases and walked to the parking garage, and were soon heading back to Chester in the Jeep.

I could see how tired they both were after the long transatlantic flight, so I decided to keep quiet about my experience on the water the day before, and my breakfast meeting that morning with Mrs. Moore.

Kate often told me she'd felt like a crazy person last Christmas when she believed I could be her long lost daughter.

Today, I felt a little crazy myself.

I waited until we finished dinner that evening to bring up the subject that had been weighing heavily on my mind since the previous day.

Kate stood up to start clearing away the dishes, but I stopped her with my hand. "Wait. Can you stay for a minute?"

"I'll take care of this," Ryan said, obviously sensing that I wanted to talk to Kate about something important. He rose to his feet as well.

"No, please stay. I want you to hear this, too."

He regarded me with curiosity.

I leaned back in my chair and turned to Kate. "This is going to sound completely insane, and I hate to do this to you when you just got home from your honeymoon, but I met someone yesterday, and I had a weird feeling about it."

Kate's eyebrows pulled together. "What kind of feeling?"

I didn't know how, or where, to begin, so I took a deep breath and did my best to explain. "A crew member on one of the boats entered in the race this week got sick, so I was asked to help out on a practice run."

I paused, and Kate sat forward, resting her elbows on the table.

"Strangely enough," I continued, "it was a family from your neck of the woods. Bar Harbor. The captain of the boat is a senator. You probably know of him. Gerald Moore?"

Kate's face lit up. "Yes! They're like royalty in Maine. The senator has a reputation for being tough but fair, and he and his wife support every worthy cause out there. They adopted a child from Somalia a number of years ago, and I wouldn't be surprised if he ends up president one day." Kate smiled at me and touched my hand. "*You sailed with the Moores yesterday?* That's incredible."

I felt almost dizzy, because what I was about to suggest was going to come as a great shock to Kate, and all at once, I was tempted to backpedal. Maybe I should just let it be. Let bygones be bygones.

But the senator would only be in Chester for another week at most, and I couldn't keep something like this secret from Kate. If it *was* true, she needed to know.

And I knew, in my heart, that Kate was strong. She had survived the deaths of her sister, her husband, and her unborn child. She could handle this, too, and anything else that came her way.

"I'm not sure how to tell you this," I said, "but it's about the senator's children. Yesterday I met Adam, the boy they adopted from Somalia. He's twenty-seven now. And I met his two sisters, Becky and Diana. They're both amazing. Diana is the older one. She's in law school at UCLA, and Becky is the youngest. She's brilliant, and she was just accepted to Oxford. She says she wants to be a classics professor. She's starting her masters in September and plans to do a PhD after that."

"That's great," Kate said, still leaning forward over the table.

A lump formed in my throat, and I couldn't seem to find the right words to suggest what I thought might be true. "Kate…" I said, "Becky is really beautiful. She's exactly my age. She has red hair, just like yours, and she's adopted."

Kate stared at me intently for a long moment, then she leaned back in her chair and frowned. "What are you saying?"

I covered her hand with my own. "This morning, I got up early and had breakfast with Mrs. Moore. She's a wonderful person. I hope you won't be angry with me, but I asked her about her daughters. I told her I knew they were adopted – it was on the Internet – and I was curious about where they came from. She was very honest with me, and said that Becky's real mother was only sixteen when she had her, and that she intended to give her baby up for adoption. She was involved in a car accident, however, and went into a long-term coma. Becky was taken to a private adoption agency in Boston."

I couldn't tear my eyes away from Kate's as all the color drained from her face. "The Moore's were on a waiting list to adopt a third child," I continued, "so they were called in."

Kate wet her lips and spoke in a shaky voice. "Do they know the name...of the mother?"

I shook my head. "The files were sealed. She didn't even know if the mother ever woke up from the coma. But she did tell me the name of the agency."

Kate laid a hand on her chest and stood up. Then she bent forward, as if she were going to be sick.

In a flash of movement, Ryan was at her side. "Are you okay? Can I get you anything?"

"I'm fine," she said. "I just need to sit down."

He went with her to the sofa, and I took a seat in the upholstered chair across from them.

"What can I do?" I said. "Was I right to tell you? I wasn't sure."

"Yes, you did the right thing," she replied, resting her forehead on the heels of her hands, "but I don't know what to do. I've been through this before. I fought hard to put it behind me and be happy in the present."

"That will never change," I said, "but I think you need to get to the bottom of this, Kate. Is there any way you can unseal the files?"

She looked up at me with animosity in her eyes. "I'm not sure," she said, "because I wasn't the one who sealed them."

Seventy-two

༄ ཙ ༂

Kate

I took a few minutes to collect myself after Marissa told me about Becky Moore, then I went into the bedroom to call my father.

Unfortunately, there was no answer. Or maybe he got call display so he could ignore me. It wouldn't be the first time.

I called many times over the next few hours, but no one answered. Worn out from jet lag and travel fatigue, eventually I could do nothing but collapse into bed with a goal to call the adoption agency first thing in the morning.

I was up at five and it was torture to wait until normal business hours in Connecticut. When at last I dialed the number, I was relieved when a real person, Ms. Bowers, answered.

I told her who I was, and explained everything.

I scanned my birth certificate and emailed it to her, along with a written document with my signature, requesting access to the files.

When she compared my signature to the original documents, she told me it didn't match.

I found a letter my father had written to me years ago with his signature on it, scanned it, and sent it by email.

I waited a long time for her to reply. When she finally called, she informed me that they suspected my signature had been forged. They would be contacting the authorities to investigate my father's actions, and Ms. Bowers suggested I speak to a lawyer.

It was not easy to comprehend that what I had suspected all my life was true: My child was alive. She had survived the accident, and I was never crazy for believing it. My instincts as a mother were real, and it shocked me to realize that she may have been living in my hometown the entire time – if in fact she was Rebecca Moore. I still did not have confirmation.

Had we ever passed each other on the street? Did we ever sit in the same theater and watch the same movie? How many times had I stumbled across her picture in the paper and read about the prestigious Moore family from Bar Harbor? If she was my daughter, how could I not have recognized her?

These were questions I could not answer. All I knew was that the young woman who could be my daughter was here in Nova Scotia, not far from me, *now*, and my darling, beloved stepdaughter, Marissa, had been the one to find her.

Once I recovered from the shock of learning the truth – and stopped crying tears of joy over the fact that my baby was alive – I had to wrap my head around the fact that my father had betrayed me in the worst possible way and had been lying to me for over twenty years.

Had my mother known? I wondered furiously as I stood on the back deck, squeezing the railing, squinting into the morning sun rising over the horizon.

No, surely that wasn't possible. For the most part, my mother had been a submissive wife, but when push came to shove, she stood up for what was right. She never forced me to have the abortion. Somehow she convinced Dad to let me have my baby.

No, this was something he must have done on his own. He had lied to her, too.

My vision clouded, and a twitchy feeling reached my extremities. I had always considered myself to be a calm, level-headed woman, and I took great pride in my self-control in emergency situations. In that moment, however, I wanted to scream and hit something – my father, specifically. I wanted to see blood. It was a good thing he was many miles away, or my mug shot might have ended up on the 6:00 news.

Thank God for cell phones, because I really needed to blow a gasket, and he, of all people, deserved to be hit by some flying emotional debris.

I went back inside, pulled my phone out of my purse, and keyed in his number. Naturally, there was no answer, so I decided, with a rather perverse sense of pleasure, to leave a nasty voicemail.

"*Dad*! You really should pick up the phone once in a while, because you have a lot of explaining to do." I clenched my jaw. "Sometimes, you know, karma comes back to bite you in the ass, and I'm calling to give you fair warning. I know what you did. I know because she's *here*. She's here in Chester, where I live. I called the adoption agency in Boston and they –"

Beep! 'If you are satisfied with your message…'

"*Shit! Are you kidding me?*" I lowered the phone from my ear and pounded my index finger over the screen to redial my father's number.

Ring, ring…

Still, no answer. I was pacing like a rabid animal by now. I wanted to strangle someone.

Again, I was directed to voicemail.

"Dad!" I shouted. "I know you've been lying to me, and I swear to God, I will never forgive you for this. I know who she is, and I know about how you forged my signature on the papers. How could you do that? How could you tell me she was dead? Especially after losing Mia! How could you give away your only grandchild? Did your reputation mean more to you than your own flesh and blood? My God, if Mom was alive today to learn about this, I can't imagine what she would think. I can't even speak right now, I am so angry with you. I have to go. Bye."

I ended the call and slammed my phone down on the granite countertop in the kitchen.

For a long while I stared at it, breathing hard while adrenaline sparked and fired through my bloodstream.

That felt good, but I knew at some point, I would need to face Dad in person.

What would I have done without Marissa? I can't begin to imagine.

That afternoon, when I was beside myself with indecision about how I should handle the situation, Marissa suggested that I allow her to contact Mrs. Moore on my behalf and ask to meet her for a drink. Marissa was willing to be my liaison with the senator's family, and said she would gently probe into what they might, or might not want.

Mrs. Moore graciously accepted Marissa's invitation, and Ryan and I waited at home for more than two hours. We turned on the television but I couldn't seem to concentrate on anything. It was the longest two hours of my life.

Then my cell phone vibrated, and I received a text from Marissa.

Hey Kate. I hope you're decent. Mrs. Moore and I are on our way over right now. Becky is with us.

I think I might have swallowed my gum. I sat forward on the sofa and handed the phone to Ryan. He read the text, and looked up at me with a smile.

"Are you ready for this?"

"I don't know," I replied, laying a hand over my heart. "What if it's all a big mistake? What if she's not really my daughter? Mrs. Bowers wouldn't tell me anything. And Lord knows, this has happened before." I shut my eyes and tried to catch my breath. "I wish I could be as calm as you are."

He shook his head. "I'm not that calm. But I think this could be a really good thing, no matter how it turns out. One way or another, you're going to have an answer tonight. We hope."

Seeing the wisdom in his optimism, I stood up and went to change out of my leggings and oversized sweatshirt. It wasn't easy to choose an outfit. *Should I wear a skirt? Heels?* Mrs. Moore was the wife of a senator. What would she be wearing?

For at least five minutes, I rifled through my closet. In the end, I settled on a casual olive-colored skirt with a black T-shirt, and flat brown leather sandals. I combed my hair, brushed my teeth, and put on some clear lip gloss.

Looking at my reflection in the mirror, I did not see the woman I was today. I saw the sixteen-year-old girl I was twenty years ago, when I took a pregnancy test in my bathroom and collapsed on the floor from the shock of the result.

I was still that same girl, and I was about to meet my daughter for the first time.

The sound of a car pulling into the driveway sent my heart into a frenzy. Voices reached me through the open window in the bathroom, as car doors opened and closed.

As I waited in the kitchen for Ryan to greet Marissa and our guests at the door, I feared my cheeks, and all the rest of me, might burst into flames.

I listened with hyper-sensitive ears to the sound of the front door opening. Ryan greeted everyone in his usual friendly manner.

"Hi, you must be Sandra. And you're Becky?"

"Yes, it's nice to meet you."

Becky's voice shot right through me, and I wondered why I was waiting here in the kitchen to be introduced. It was making the anticipation that much more unbearable.

Oh, but how grateful I was for Ryan's calm and charismatic presence at the door. Without seeing the faces of our guests, I knew he was putting everyone at ease.

"Come on in," he said, and they entered the front hall. "I hear you're competing this week. Marissa said you have a champion of a boat."

I assumed it was Mrs. Moore who replied. "That's quite a compliment. We certainly enjoyed having Marissa on board yesterday. She's a top-notch sailor. You must be very proud of her."

Ryan paused. "Yeah, well..." He paused. "She's all right, I guess."

Becky laughed boisterously – at least I think it was Becky – and I heard the sound of Marissa punching Ryan in the arm.

"Ouch!" he said, chuckling.

They began moving toward the kitchen, and every second felt earth-shatteringly slow to me...until at last, I saw their faces.

~~⌒~~

It was exactly how I imagined it would be. The moment I laid eyes on Becky Moore, I knew she was my daughter. It was like seeing another version of myself as a young woman. The physical similarities were uncanny. She had many of the same features as me – the upturned nose, the freckled complexion, and suddenly I understood what people meant when they said I had compelling eyes. Her hair was thick, wavy, and red like mine, and her smile was almost disconcerting to behold.

I was surprised that I felt no anger, no regret, no compulsion to fall apart and weep over all the lost years. I felt nothing but euphoria to see my adult daughter so full of spirit and happiness. I knew at once that she'd had a wonderful life. For the first time I actually believed that the deep fracture in my heart might begin to heal.

She was alive. My baby. And she was beautiful.

When my heart floated back down to the ground, I realized Ryan was standing beside me with his hand on the small of my back. "Sandra, Becky...this is my wife, Kate. Kate, this is Sandra and Becky Moore."

I moved to shake their hands. I'm not sure what I expected, but I was thankful this wasn't escalating into a histrionic, emotional scene where we would hug each other and weep uncontrollably. That would have been difficult to bear.

Not to understate the drama that was playing out inside of me – my heart was pounding thunderously. I was mesmerized and speechless.

All my life I had dreamed of finding my baby. Now, here she was, in the flesh, in my home, shaking my hand.

Marissa moved to stand beside Becky. "This is strange, isn't it," she said, breaking the ice with a strangely graceful sledgehammer. I loved her for it.

My gaze locked with Mrs. Moore's. Her eyes were warm and smiling, as if we shared a common secret. To my surprise, I wanted to rush into *her* arms and hug her and weep like a baby.

"It certainly is," Sandra said. "You have no idea how many times we wished we could find out what happened to you, and wished we knew more about you. We never imagined you were from our own hometown."

"I was curious about you, too," I replied.

"No, you don't understand," she continued, moving toward me to clasp both my hands in hers. "I'm so relieved to finally know that you didn't die in that accident. You have no idea how we dreamed of a moment like this, how we talked about it. Becky always said she was certain you survived. She never stopped believing it, and she was sure that one day, somehow, we would find you."

So much for polite, genteel greetings. A flood of emotion welled up inside me, and my eyes filled with tears. "I never believed you were dead either."

Before I could take another breath, Becky walked into my arms. Suddenly we were embracing each other. Blinking in disbelief, I felt the beat of her heart against my chest; I breathed in the clean natural fragrance of her skin. Oh, God, it was the answer to all my prayers.

I felt reborn.

I never had the chance to hold her when she was a baby, to press my nose to her soft, tiny head, or watch her clasp my finger in her little palm, but how many times had I dreamed of it?

This moment was everything I'd ever wanted, and more – because now I knew that she had been dreaming of this, too. All her life.

"I'm so happy to finally meet you," I managed to say through shaky breaths. "I feel so lucky – to know that you found a good family."

"They found me," she said with a smile that moved me deeply as she drew back and looked into my eyes. I was spellbound.

"Thank you for unsealing the files," Sandra said. "I was able to call the agency as soon as Marissa told me what happened. They confirmed everything."

"They unsealed the files?"

"You didn't know?"

I shook my head. "Maybe they weren't sure of the legal issues," I suggested. "I think they're afraid I'm going to sue them."

"You would have every right to," she replied. "What happened was…unthinkable. I give you my word that Gerry will look into it. He'll want to make sure nothing like this ever happens again."

"I appreciate that."

Sandra paused. "I'm so sorry, Kate. If we had known the papers were forged, we never would have gone ahead with the adoption."

"I don't blame *you*," I assured her. "You did nothing wrong. You're good people, and I'm grateful that you took such good care of Becky. If you only knew how many times I prayed that she was alive, and if she was, that she was with a family just like yours."

Ryan offered drinks to all of us. While he and Marissa mixed up a pitcher of iced tea, the rest of us moved into the living room.

Becky sat down beside me. "There's so much I want to know about you," she said. "Marissa tells me you were a paramedic."

I nodded and told her about my career in New Hampshire. One thing led to another, and soon everything came out – how I almost had an abortion but changed my mind at the last minute, how Glenn and I were married right after high school, how we weren't able to have any more children, and how he eventually became involved with some bad people. That brought us to the reason why, and how, I ended up in Chester.

"First of all," Becky said, "thank you for walking out of the abortion clinic that day. I'm happy you decided to have me, or I wouldn't be here. That was very brave of you."

"I think I had some sort of vision of you," I replied, "because I saw a little red-haired girl, and I heard her laughing. Now here you are, with red hair and an infectious laugh. It's so strange to think about."

We all fell silent, but there was no awkwardness to it.

"Maybe this was how it was always meant to be," I said, "because I was so young. I'm not positive I would have been the best parent for you."

"I'm sure you would have been great," Becky said, taking hold of my hand and squeezing it.

I regarded her with warmth and appreciation. "You've had a good life, and I can see how much your mom loves you, and how you love her. I can't lie. I'll always be angry with my father for what he did, but when I look at you now, I feel very blessed to know that you had the life I always wanted for you. I wished on every star, and now I can't help but believe that dreams and wishes do come true, and miracles do happen."

"Kate." Marissa gave me a look as she set down the tray of iced tea. "Speaking of miracles…"

I didn't understand at first, and then I remembered.

❝I s this yours?" Kate asked Becky.

Sandra gasped and covered her mouth with a hand, while Becky stood up from her chair. "Oh, my. Where did you find him?"

"I'm not sure, exactly," Marissa said, "because it was my grandmother who found him, and she passed away last Christmas. But it must have been somewhere in the village. She brought him home to me one day and said he was an orphan, and that he needed a good home."

Becky took Bubba into her arms and turned to her mother.

"We lost him years ago," Sandra said, "when we sailed up here for the summer. We searched everywhere for him, and whenever we came back, we always hoped we'd stumble across him somehow. But he was with you all along? How in the world did you know he belonged to *Becky*?"

"Because he used to belong to *me,*" I replied. "He was with me in the ambulance when I had the accident, and the only explanation I can give is that my father did at least one thing right. When he took you to the agency, he must have made sure Bubba went with you. The only question I had was how Bubba ended up here in Chester. When Marissa heard that your family had been coming here from Bar Harbor for years, that's what made her think about the connections."

Though I would always resent my father for what he did, I decided in that moment that I would choose to be grateful for that one small gesture on his part. He had made sure that a part of me stayed with my baby.

Becky hugged Bubba tight to her chest, and again, her smile and laughter moved right through me.

Epilogue

I am not sure how to finish my story, because it isn't truly finished. I still live in Chester with Ryan, and I am in awe of the world and all the magic that happens around us. I look up at the sky and marvel at the clouds. I'm moved by the beauty of the sun reflecting off the water like thousands of shimmering diamonds. How lucky we all are to be surrounded by such magnificence.

I also marvel at Ryan's handsome profile when we are driving in the car, going somewhere we've never been before. I'm filled with joy each time he smiles at me or takes my hand in his.

I'll never regret the fact that I was pregnant as a teenager, and I will always believe it was my destiny to love Glenn. Nor will I forget that I was forced to say good-bye to many people I loved. It's a lot of grief for one person to carry. There was a time I was bitter about all I lost. It seemed very unfair.

But here I am today, married to an incredible man who loves me with a passion and devotion I can barely fathom. His love is mind-boggling to me, yet I return it with equal measure.

These days, Marissa is busy starting a psychiatry residency in Ottawa. She'll be specializing in geriatrics. She married Sean two years ago, and he works for the Federal Government. They hope to eventually return to Nova Scotia and raise a family here.

Becky spent a few summers with us in Chester, working at the yacht club as a sailing instructor. She stayed in Gladys's apartment downstairs, and she and I were able to catch up on some of what we missed over the past twenty years.

But let me reiterate: I never surrendered to regret. My glass is half-full, not half-empty. The way I see it, our separation was only for the *first* twenty years. There is still so much living left to do. Things left to discover and enjoy.

When Becky finished her doctorate at Oxford, she accepted a position at King's College in Halifax – only an hour away from us – teaching Classics in the Foundation Year Program. I sometimes smile at the thought that she chose to major in the arts, not science, while my stepdaughter, Marissa, not biologically related to me in any way, is the medical geek. It just goes to show that our children are not carbon copies of us, even if we imagine that is how they will turn out. They have their own souls; they choose their own paths.

Becky is happy and fulfilled in her work. She visits often, and last year, she met a wonderful man who owns a winery in the valley. They just got engaged, so Ryan and I have our fingers crossed that in time, when Marissa comes home, we'll be blessed with a house full of grandchildren.

As for my father, I never saw him again, though he did leave one voicemail on my phone: 'I did you a favor, and you know it. And I did that kid a favor. You should be thanking me.'

Ryan and I, together with the Moore's, were considering our options about charging him with fraud, when he died of a heart attack. It happened about a month after I was reunited with

Becky. His neighbor called to tell me that he collapsed in his kitchen. He was alone at the time.

Do I feel guilty about the nasty voicemail I left? Sometimes, yes. I wonder what might have occurred if I'd been less confrontational. Maybe he would have expressed some remorse. I will never know, however, so that is something I must live with.

I will finish now with this thought: Sometimes life is cruel, and it can seem pointless and tragic. But occasionally – surprisingly – certain hardships can lead you down a new path you never dreamed possible.

Maybe that new path was your destiny all along. And when you look back, you do so with acceptance, forgiveness, and peace.

I hope you find the path you are meant to be on. If you haven't yet, it may be just over the next rise.

Or if you have found it, I hope it is everything you dreamed it would be.

Questions for Discussion

1. In the Prologue, Kate says 'I've often wondered if a person's life follows a path that is laid out long before he or she ever takes a first step. Or are we in control of what happens to us?' What do you believe is the answer to this question, and how much control did Kate have over her fate in the end?

2. In Chapter Seven, Kate's mother says, 'You're only fifteen, Kate. There will be plenty of other boys.' Do you believe it's possible for a fifteen-year-old girl to know that she's found her mate for life? Do you think Kate was foolish to believe this? Why or why not?

3. If there had been no ambulance accident, and Kate had her baby according to plan, do you think her father would have kept his promise and allowed her to marry Glenn? Would the marriage have been a success?

4. When 'Elizabeth' makes her first appearance at Ryan's house, had you forgotten about Kate's story? At what point in the novel did you begin to suspect that Elizabeth and Kate might be the same woman?

5. Do you think Gladys met Becky years earlier? What might have happened? How, or why, did Bubba end up with Marissa?

6. Kate chooses to remember her father's kind act of making sure that her teddy bear went with Becky to the adoption clinic. Is this a form of forgiveness on her part, and do you believe he deserves it? How did you feel about what happened with her father in the end? Would you have preferred to see things end differently between them? How? And why?

7. In what ways are Kate and Ryan mirror images of each other? How does this relate to the idea of soul mates?

8. What is the significance of the woman from the lake? Kate never learns if she wakes from her coma. Why do you think the author chose to leave that question unanswered for Kate?

9. What are the key themes in the novel? Can you provide a few examples of where the themes are conveyed through the characters' dialogue or introspection?

10. Do you believe in miracles or real life magic? Or is it all luck and coincidence?

11. Are there any events in your life that seem pre-destined? Why do you believe this?

For more information about this book and others in the Color of Heaven series, please visit the author's website at www. juliannemaclean.com. While you're there be sure to sign up for Julianne's newsletter to be notified about when a new book in this series is released.

Read on for an excerpt from *The Color of Hope*, book three in the Color of Heaven Series.

Excerpt from

The COLOR *of* HOPE

Book Three
Available Now

Diana Moore has led a charmed life. She's the daughter of a wealthy senator and living a glamorous city life, and is confident her handsome live-in boyfriend is about to propose. But everything is turned upside down when she learns of a mysterious woman who lives and works nearby – a woman who is her exact mirror image.

Diana is compelled to discover the truth about this woman's identity, but the truth leads her down a path of secrets, betrayals, and shocking discoveries about her past. These discoveries follow her like a shadow.

Then she meets Dr. Jacob Peterson—a brilliant cardiac surgeon with an uncanny ability to heal those who are broken. With his help, Diana embarks upon a journey to restore her belief in the human spirit, and recover a sense of hope - that happiness, and love, may still be within reach for those willing to believe in second chances.

❧

Nadia Carmichael

Have you ever done something you wish you could undo? What am I saying? Of course you have. Everyone has regrets. Some are just more life changing than others, and some go beyond a single moment of carelessness. Some regrets are born out over a period of months, or even years of misbehavior, because you didn't have enough self-awareness or life experience to recognize the error you were making at the time.

For me, the greatest mistake of my life resulted in a shock one autumn morning when I was twenty-seven years old and couldn't hold down my breakfast.

"Are you all right in there?" Rick asked, pounding hard on the bathroom door. "I need to get in. I'm going to be late for work."

I moved to the sink to splash water on my face and swig some Scope, which I swished around in my mouth from cheek to cheek. "I'm almost done," I replied, wiping my mouth with a tissue I'd pulled from the gleaming – and no doubt expensive – silver-plated dispenser. "I'll be right out."

I paused to take a breath and calm the sickening sensation of panic that rose from my belly to my chest.

Or was it really panic? Maybe it was nervous excitement. If this wasn't a flu bug or food poisoning, and I was actually pregnant – *pregnant* – what would it mean for my future?

By the time I collected myself and emerged from the bathroom, Rick had moved on. He was no longer pounding on the door.

I padded softly across the polished hardwood floor to the kitchen, where I found him with his back to me at the cappuccino maker.

"The bathroom's free," I mentioned as I slid onto one of the high stools at the kitchen bar.

"Thanks." He picked up his coffee cup and disappeared down the hall.

I heard the sound of the bathroom door closing and the water running.

By the time he finished showering, I was dressed and heading out the door to work. "See you tonight," I called out, and went straight to the pharmacy to buy a pregnancy test.

That night, I picked up some groceries to cook dinner for Rick. Not that I had much of an appetite. I'd felt queasy all day, which wasn't easy to cope with because I worked as a receptionist in a law firm in downtown LA, and my face was the first thing clients saw when they walked through the door. The pay wasn't great, but at least I wasn't cleaning toilets.

It was half past seven before Rick finally walked through the door. I turned on the stove and slid the wok – fully prepped with freshly chopped vegetables – onto the burner.

He entered the kitchen but didn't look up from his iPhone. "I'm here," he said. "What did you want to talk about?"

I faced him and wished he wasn't so impossibly handsome. With that athletic build and thick, dark hair, he always looked like a dream come true in his tailored black business suits. He wore suits to work every day, which always turned me into an idiotic puddle of infatuation, despite my sincere efforts to keep my head.

How could one man be so difficult to resist? There was no point questioning now. It was too late, because I'd already lost every shred of integrity I possessed when I dove head first into this terrible disaster of a relationship five months ago.

Now here we were, facing each other in his kitchen, dealing with the fallout while I feared karma was about to bite me in the ass.

"Go take off your tie and pour yourself a drink." I turned back to the stove and stirred the vegetables. "Then I'll tell you all about it."

I deserved what was about to come my way, I told myself as I spooned the stir fry onto two plates and carried them to the table. I knew, before I sat down, exactly how this was going to play out. Rick might be every woman's romantic fantasy – because he was a drop-dead-gorgeous professional who earned millions, and when he looked at you, he made you feel like the most beautiful woman alive – but that's where the dream ended. He had made it clear on countless occasions that he wasn't the marrying kind. He wasn't looking for a lifetime commitment. It's part of the reason why we ended up together. He enjoyed the fact that I had plucked him out of a suffocating relationship, even though I had destroyed my own happiness in the process.

'Thank God for you,' he whispered in my ear one night on an elevator. 'You're the escape hatch I need.'

I am ashamed by how those words seduced me, and how happy I was to be anything at all to him.

After setting both plates down on the candlelit table, I poured myself a glass of sparkling water.

"You're not having wine?" Rick asked as he stood up from the computer chair to join me.

"Not in the mood," I replied, formulating how I was going to explain why.

I decided to eat first. I'd let him finish that glass of wine.

Then I would drop the bomb.

Three

⌐⌐⌐⌐⌐

"I beg your pardon?" Rick's eyebrows lifted. He set his glass down, wiped his mouth with a napkin, and leaned back in his chair.

An ambulance siren wailed in the street below his luxury high rise condo, but I was not disconcerted by it, or by the fact that he was clearly shocked and displeased. There was a time I might have crumbled and wept over the loss of a man's attentions and begged for a second chance – but after what I had done to reach this juncture in my life, I was astoundingly calm and firmly braced for the oncoming rejection. I expected it. Perhaps I even *wanted* it – because I needed to believe there was some justice in the world.

"I'm pregnant," I said. I gave him a few seconds to digest my words before I continued. "I threw up this morning, in case you didn't notice. So I took a test on my lunch hour."

He stared at me with those spellbinding blue eyes. "I thought you were on the pill."

"I was," I explained. "I don't know what happened. I didn't forget to take any."

He frowned at me. "You must have. You were careless and forgot. Or you're lying. Maybe you wanted this."

"No," I argued, dropping my fork with a noisy clank onto my plate. "I didn't do this on purpose. Our relationship has enough bad blood in it to begin with. I wouldn't dare add any more poison."

His eyes narrowed. "How am I supposed to trust you? *You?*"

Rage, hot and brisk, flooded my bloodstream. How dare he suggest that I was the one who caused all the hurt, as if I were a wicked siren who seduced and lured him into this wreckage. I wiped my mouth with the linen napkin and threw it onto the table. "That's the pot calling the kettle black, don't you think?"

"Is it?" He shoved his chair back and rose to his feet. "I feel like a damned trout that was flipped around in a frying pan and tossed into the fire. And you know what I'm talking about."

I picked up my plate and carried it to the sink. My chest was heaving, as if I'd just climbed ten flights of stairs.

I hate you. I wanted to say that and more as I ran the water and rinsed my plate, because I blamed him for everything – for the inconceivable magnitude of my disgrace. For the destruction and collapse of this new world that could have been so good for me. Five months ago, I'd been blessed with a miracle, but I threw it all away for the dream of being with a sophisticated man with money.

Why?

Was I that shallow? That much in need of security? That weak to temptation? That self-destructive? And if so, was it really my fault that I had turned out this way? How much bad luck could one woman take before losing touch with her soul?

Or maybe I was just shifting the blame. Maybe I had to accept the fact that I'd screwed up a lot of things recently, and this was my comeuppance.

"It doesn't matter if I forgot to take the pill," I said. "But I didn't. All we can do is move on. We have to decide how we're going to handle this." I shut off the faucet, set my plate in the dishwasher, and made my way back to the table.

Rick sank back into his chair. "You're sure?" he said. "Maybe you should go to the doctor to get it confirmed."

I shook my head. "A positive test result is over ninety-five percent accurate. I'm pregnant, Rick. It's a fact. I know it wasn't something either of us planned, but this is where we are. So what are we going to do?"

It's rather unfortunate, don't you think, that some people are dealt a bad hand in life?

At the same time, I don't want to suggest that we have no control over the road we choose to take, or that we shouldn't accept full responsibility for our attitudes and actions. I will be the first person to stand up and say that our past does not have to dictate our future. It's what we do *now*, in this moment, moving forward that counts.

So if I'm going to take you forward – or backward as the case may be – and seek your understanding, I should at least share with you the events that wrestled me into this situation in the first place. That way, when you hear the *other* side of this story, maybe you'll be able to forgive me for what I did, and the choices I made.

The first card of misfortune dealt to me was the untimely death of my birth mother, who suffered a stroke during delivery. My biological father was married to another woman at the time, so I was promptly shuffled off to an adoption agency.

My second bad luck card came a week later when I was diagnosed with a septal defect, more commonly referred to as a hole in the heart. It usually resolves itself naturally, but in 1983, the state of New York required adoption agencies to reveal an adoptee's medical records to prospective parents. My chances of finding a family with open arms were therefore diminished, because no one wanted a kid with the possibility of a giant medical bill attached to her future.

I spent months in the hospital, and was then placed in foster care while the agency waited for my heart to heal.

I have no memory of my first few years, but I shudder to think about how distressing it must have been for me to be pulled from the loving warmth of my mother's womb and not understand, intellectually, the concept of her death. Did I grieve for the loss of her on that day and in the coming months? Did anyone pick me up, hold me, talk to me, or make me feel loved? Or did I lay alone, untouched, in a sterile white crib?

I don't know the answers to those questions and probably never will. But based on my behavior as an adult woman and how I dealt with relationships, I suspect that I missed out on the sort of bonding experience that shapes most children whose mothers don't die in childbirth.

I was four years old when someone finally adopted me, and for better or worse, I became part of a new family.

My mother worked as a maid in a Washington DC hotel that catered to visiting civil servants and politicians. My father was a bricklayer with a drinking problem.

Their divorce was finalized when I was nine, which was probably for the best, because I spent far too much time hiding under my bed when they argued. The sound of my mother's shrieking voice filled me with dread because she never backed down from a fight and always called my father out when he blew the entire week's grocery budget at the tavern on payday.

My father wasn't talkative. He responded to her complaints with the back of his hand. To this day, I still jump at the sound of breaking glass or a lamp being knocked over in another room.

After my father left, Mom and I lived in our tiny apartment for a few years, until Dad stopped paying child support. That's when everything began to spin out of control.

OTHER BOOKS IN THE
COLOR OF HEAVEN SERIES

The COLOR *of* HEAVEN

Book One
Available Now

A deeply emotional tale about Sophie Duncan, a successful columnist whose world falls apart after her daughter's unexpected illness and her husband's shocking affair. When it seems nothing else could possibly go wrong, her car skids off an icy road and plunges into a frozen lake. There, in the cold dark depths of the water, a profound and extraordinary experience unlocks the surprising secrets from Sophie's past, and teaches her what it means to truly live…and love.

Full of surprising twists and turns and a near-death experience that will leave you breathless, this story is not to be missed.

"A gripping, emotional tale you'll want to read in one sitting."
—*New York Times* bestselling author, Julia London

"Brilliantly poignant mainstream tale."
—4½ starred review, *Romantic Times*

The COLOR of A DREAM

Book Four
Available Now

Nadia Carmichael has had a lifelong run of bad luck. It begins on the day she is born, when she is separated from her identical twin sister and put up for adoption. Twenty-seven years later, not long after she is finally reunited with her twin and is expecting her first child, Nadia falls victim to a mysterious virus and requires a heart transplant.

Now recovering from the surgery with a new heart, Nadia is haunted by a recurring dream that sets her on a path to discover the identity of her donor. Her efforts are thwarted, however, when the father of her baby returns to sue for custody of their child. It's not until Nadia learns of his estranged brother Jesse that she begins to explore the true nature of her dreams, and discover what her new heart truly needs and desires…

The COLOR of A MEMORY

Book Five
Available Now

ER nurse Audrey Fitzgerald believed she was married to the perfect man - a heroic firefighter who saved lives, even beyond his own death. But a year after losing him she meets a mysterious woman who has some unexplained connection to her husband...

Soon Audrey discovers that in the weeks leading up to her husband's death, he was keeping secrets, and she wonders if she ever really knew him at all. Compelled to dig into his past and explore memories that define the essence of their relationship, Audrey embarks upon a journey of discovery that will lead her down a new path to the future - a future she never dared to imagine.

The COLOR of LOVE

Book Six
Available Now

Carla Matthews is a single mother struggling to make ends meet and give her daughter Kaleigh a decent upbringing. When Kaleigh's absent father Seth—a famous alpine climber who never wanted to be tied down—begs for a second chance at fatherhood, Carla is hesitant because she doesn't want to pin her hopes on a man who is always seeking another mountain to scale. A man who was never willing to stay put in one place and raise a family. But when Seth's plane goes missing after a crash landing in the harsh Canadian wilderness, Carla must wait for news…Is he dead or alive? Will the wreckage ever be found?

One year later, after having given up all hope, Carla receives a shocking phone call. A man has been found, half-dead, floating on an iceberg in the North Atlantic, uttering her name. Is this Seth? And is it possible that he will come home to her and Kaleigh at last, and be the man she always dreamed he would be?

The Color of the Season: Book Seven
Available November 2014

The Color of Joy: Book Eight
Available February 2015

Praise for Julianne MacLean's
bestselling romances

"It takes a talented author to segue from a lighthearted tale of seduction to an emotionally powerful romance that plays on your heartstrings…a very special, powerful read."
—*Romantic Times Book Reviews*

"Julianne has the ability to transport the reader."
—*Once Upon a Romance*

"Five hearts…a special kind of love story…truly compelling."
—*The Romance Reader*

"A box of tissues should be included in the purchase price of this book…. I finished The Color of Heaven in a matter of hours, but I've no doubt the read and the lessons imparted through Sophie's story will stay with me…probably forever. The Color of Heaven is an incredibly poignant and unbelievably gripping novel, deserving Romance Junkies' highest rating."
—*Romance Junkies*

"A gripping, emotional tale you'll want to read in one sitting."
—*New York Times* bestselling author, Julia London

"Brilliantly poignant mainstream tale."
—*Romantic Times*

About the Author

Julianne MacLean is a *USA Today* bestselling author of many historical romances, including The Highlander Series with St. Martin's Press and her popular American Heiress Series with Avon/Harper Collins. She also writes contemporary mainstream fiction, and The Color of Heaven was *a USA Today* bestseller. She is a three-time RITA finalist, and has won numerous awards, including the Booksellers' Best Award, the Book Buyer's Best Award, and a Reviewers' Choice Award from Romantic Times for Best Regency Historical of 2005. She lives in Nova Scotia with her husband and daughter, and is a dedicated member of Romance Writers of Atlantic Canada.

Please visit Julianne's website for more information about her books and writing life, and while you're there, be sure to sign up for her reader newsletter to stay informed about upcoming books and special events.

Made in the USA
Lexington, KY
26 March 2016